WAFFLES AND SCUFFLES

AN IVY CREEK COZY MYSTERY

RUTH BAKER

CLEANTALES PUBLISHING

Copyright © CleanTales Publishing

First published in April 2022

All characters and events in this publication, other than those clearly in the public domain, are fictitious and any resemblance to real persons, living or dead, is purely coincidental.

Copyright © CleanTales Publishing

The moral right of the author has been asserted.

All rights reserved. This book or any portion thereof may not be reproduced or used in any manner whatsoever without the express written permission of the publisher except for the use of brief quotations in a book review.

For questions and comments about this book, please contact
info@cleantales.com

ISBN: 9798441596145
Imprint: Independently Published

OTHER BOOKS IN THE IVY CREEK SERIES

Which Pie Goes with Murder?
Twinkle, Twinkle, Deadly Sprinkles
Eat Once, Die Twice
Silent Night, Unholy Bites
Waffles and Scuffles

AN IVY CREEK COZY MYSTERY

BOOK FIVE

1

Lucy unwound the lights from the celling board frames and dropped them into the box her Aunt Tricia held. When she stepped down from the chair, she dusted her palms together and sighed.

"That's all of it," she said, and looked around the store.

They had just finished taking down the Christmas decorations, and now the bakery's dining area was back to its regular look.

Lucy smiled as she looked around, hands propped on her hips. "Seems like the place is back to its old self, and we might need something new to spark things up for the new year."

"Maybe a new addition to the menu? Like the waffles you made for your delivery today," Aunt Tricia said as she was closing the box.

"That sounds like a brilliant idea," Lucy responded as she walked over to the counter. It was still the first week of the new year, and she had just re-opened the bakery. There was a lot she had on her list for the new year, and one of them had been expanding Sweet Delights.

"Maybe waffles and another kind of cupcake? I'm thinking cheesecake," Aunt Tricia was saying as she carried the box into the adjoining office and came back out.

Lucy had pulled out her notepad and was now scribbling down the idea her aunt suggested.

"It's a new year, so we should start out with something new to excite the customers. I love the waffles idea…" Lucy closed the notepad and looked at her aunt. "Personally, I also have some new goals for the new year."

"Really? Like what?" Aunt Tricia asked as she pulled a chair towards herself. The bakery had opened for the day, and they were yet to get their first customer. Lucy took the chance to sit with her aunt in the dining area. She was still expecting her friend and assistant, Hannah, and she was sure she would arrive at any moment.

"I don't know… I just think I want to find true love this year," she said, and rested her chin on both hands with her elbows balanced on the table in front of her. "The kind my parents had," she added with a wistful sigh.

The holidays had filled Lucy's mind with memories of her childhood. Her parents spent every moment together. Lucy remembered they went on brief trips during the holidays, and in those times, she had envisioned her life with her future husband being just as splendid as her parents. Her parents had died the previous year and Lucy couldn't help reminiscing about the good times she had with them.

"I always admired your mother's relationship with Tom," Aunt Tricia said, referring to Lucy's father, Tom Hale. "At first, I thought it would wear out... the way he adored her from the start, but it never did."

"I crave what they had," Lucy said as she sighed again. "Maybe I'll have what they had someday?"

"Of course, honey," Aunt Tricia replied. "I mean... what about Richard? That young man cares for you."

Lucy had been dating Richard Lester, the owner of a cafeteria, for some months now, and although she liked him; his kind personality and attentiveness... she still didn't want to rush things.

"We're still taking it slow, getting to know each other," she told her aunt.

"He seems like a real nice young man, and I think both of you should think about taking things to the next level? It's been some months now."

Lucy flushed at her aunt's statement and waved her hand dismissively. "I do like Richard. That's why we're taking it slow."

Her aunt shrugged, raising her hand in the air. "Well then, I think you don't need to worry too much about true love for now. It will come in its own good time."

Lucy was about to change the subject to something more work related when the new doorbell she had installed rang once, and the door swung open.

Hannah walked into the store alongside a customer. Lucy had made her way to the back of the counter to attend to the customer while Aunt Tricia relaxed further in her chair.

"Hey, hey," Hannah greeted as she came to where Lucy stood and hugged her briefly before greeting Aunt Tricia. "Happy new year," Hannah continued.

Lucy was smiling as she quickly attended to the customer, then went around to join Hannah and her aunt. "I haven't seen you since the start of the new year," she said as she sat down.

"I went on a holiday with my sister, and just got back. How did your holiday go?" Hannah asked.

"It went well. Oh my God, I love your new haircut," Lucy said as her eyes settled on Hannah's platinum blonde hair. She admired the pixie cut style.

Hannah smiled at her and touched some strands of it. "It's a new year, so I decided to go with a new look."

"I love it," Lucy complimented again. "It frames your face, and it makes your smile stand out."

Lucy watched Hannah look around the bakery. Her eyes settled on a basket of cupcakes and cookies she arranged on the left end of the counter.

"Are those for delivery?" Hannah asked, one brow quirking up.

"The town council is having their first meeting for the year, and I was asked to deliver some treats. I'm taking them there soon," Lucy said and glanced at the watch on her wrist.

Hannah went into the office to hang her coat and returned to the counter.

"Will you come with me to deliver the treats for the council meeting?" Lucy asked.

"Yes, sure… are you ready to go?" Hannah asked.

Aunt Tricia rose to her feet. "I'll stay here till you both get back," she said.

Lucy walked over to the table and picked up the baskets. Minutes later, she was driving down the street with Hannah, and listening to some pop song on the radio.

They passed the police station as they headed for the town hall, and Lucy saw some cops standing out front. They seemed knee-deep in their discussion, and she stared for a long time, trying to see if she would spot Taylor, the town's deputy sheriff, amongst them.

During the holidays, Lucy had spent some time with the deputy, who was her ex, before she left Ivy Creek years ago. He had frequented the store during the holiday to buy her treats almost every day.

Her relationship with Taylor had been frosty when she first arrived back in town and she didn't think it could ever get better, but recently, they were communicating better whenever they ran into each other; most of the tension that had hung in the air whenever they had bumped into each other had eased away.

"It's my first time coming here during the meeting," Hannah said when they arrived at the hall, and Lucy stepped out of the car with her. They headed towards the entrance, both holding baskets, and Lucy greeted the first woman she saw at the reception when they entered.

"Hi, I'm Lucy Hale… I'm here to deliver treats for the town's local council meeting today."

The red-haired woman behind the reception desk gave them a warm, welcoming smile. "It's a pleasure to meet you, Lucy.

I'm Judy... Judy Cousins, a member of the board," she said. "The meeting has already begun. Would you like to join us?"

Judy took the basket Lucy handed her.

"I should be on my way," she said and was about turning around when Judy stopped her with a light touch to her shoulder.

"I was hoping you would join us for the meeting," she said. "It's a good opportunity for me to introduce you to the council members."

"Uh... I didn't plan to," Lucy replied.

"Come on... like I said, it's a good opportunity. You shouldn't let it pass," Judy urged. "The meeting won't last that long."

Lucy shot Hannah a glance to know what she thought, and Hannah responded with a slight shrug.

"Alright," she agreed.

Judy led them into the main hall where other council members had already gathered, and they found a seat at the back.

Lucy and Hannah watched Judy walk away, her three-inch heels clicking against the floor as she headed to the front of the hall where some members were seated. She took a seat amongst them, crossed her fingers, and kept her hands on the desk in front of her before she began speaking.

The council members talked about the town's welfare, and near the end, Judy and some other lady shared the treats before Judy announced. "The last item on our agenda is to discuss the open auditions at the theater."

"I hope we don't have to attend?" one man asked, raising his hand from the crowd.

A few others murmured, and Judy lifted her hand to gain their attention again. "It's being organized by Pete Jenson," she announced. "He'd expect us to be there."

The mention of the name made the crowd fall into a hushed silence, and Lucy scanned the crowd. She noticed most of the council members wore concerned looks on their faces, their brows furrowed as they listened to Judy.

She turned back to Hannah and asked in a low tone as people began filing out of the hall. "Who's Pete Jenson?"

2

"Pete Jenson is Ivy Creek's famous director. Haven't you heard of him?" Hannah asked. Lucy turned to Hannah as she tucked some loose strands of hair behind her ear. "He used to run the local theater and direct plays there before he became a global star when a play he wrote and directed became a hit on Broadway. Now he has his own production company, and he's a major player in the theater industry."

Lucy shook her head. She had never heard of Pete Jenson, but she was curious to know more about him after she heard all his achievements.

"How is it I've never heard of him?" Lucy asked as she drove back to the bakery after they left the town hall.

"Let's just say he's not everyone's cup of tea. People still remember how he cut corners and left some businesses in a pickle. You probably don't know him because he changed his name. He used to go by Pete Gruden."

Lucy replayed the words in her head and wondered how many toes Pete had stepped on in his pursuit of success. She could recall the name Gruden, even though she couldn't remember the face. Her parents had to have mentioned him when they were alive.

"Judy probably mentioned that people should be wary of him because he has a reputation of going back on his word," Hannah said as they passed the traffic lights on the road next to the bakery.

"It'd be nice to meet him," she said, as she parked her car.

"I don't think it would be a good idea to," Hannah replied as she got out of the car.

They entered the bakery, and Lucy heard laughter from the doorway even before she stepped in. Taylor and her aunt sat at a table having what seemed like a friendly chat. Taylor rose to his feet when he saw her.

"Hey," she said as she got close. Her hands moved into the pocket of the coat she wore, and she stopped in front of him.

"Taylor dropped by shortly after you left and we've just been catching up."

"You dropped by for some carrot bread?" she asked.

Taylor smiled and nodded. "How did you know?"

Her eyes latched onto his for a second before she walked past him and headed to the counter.

"I know you… It's your favorite and your mother's too," she replied.

Hannah made her way into the kitchen while Lucy began packaging some carrot bread. She wrapped up a bag and handed it to Taylor over the table.

"Say hello to your mom for me," she said when he took the pack.

"I will. See you around, Lucy."

When he left the bakery, Lucy caught the mischievous gleam in her aunt's eyes that made her flush.

"He came to see you," Aunt Tricia said as she pulled on an apron and wrapped her hair into a bun. "I had to delay him a little till you got back."

Lucy shook her head. "He came for the bread, aunt. Let's not get any ideas."

Lucy kept smiling as she entered the kitchen to join Hannah. They started baking and had made three batches of cupcakes and brownies.

Aunt Tricia sat in the dining area when they entered, and Lucy joined her after getting a glass of water from the kitchen. Minutes after they arrived, Richard walked in.

Lucy dropped the napkin she wiped her hands on, went around the counter, and flung her arms around his neck.

"Happy new year," he said, bringing his hands out from behind him to hand over the flowers he held.

Richard had been away on a skiing trip with some of his friends, so they hadn't seen each other since the start of the new year.

"How are you?" he said.

"I've never been better," Lucy replied, grinning as she accepted the gift, and out of the corner of her eyes, she saw Aunt Tricia give her another knowing grin. "Give me a moment while I find a place for this."

When she returned to the dining area, she found Richard and Aunt Tricia talking. He laughed to some joke she had made, and she put her hand on his arm.

"Walk with me," Richard said when she joined them. "I've missed you, and I'd like to spend some time with you."

"Uhm… I have to stay in the bakery," she started, rubbing the back of her neck.

"Come on, Lucy… it's the first week of January. There's no customer here anyway as everyone's trying to reduce the number of sweet treats they have this time of the year," Aunt Tricia said.

Lucy's rubbed the back of her neck because of her aunt's obvious matchmaking, and she bit her lower lip.

"Just go with the gentleman already," Aunt Tricia said, chuckling this time. "I will handle things with Hannah, okay?"

There was a grin on Richard's face when she looked at him, and she gave in.

"Alright… let's walk."

Minutes later, they were strolling down the street hand in hand. A chilly wind blew in their direction, but they kept their pace, passing the first curve out of their street.

They were heading towards the town's local church when Lucy angled her head towards him. "How was your trip?"

Richard looked at her and tightened his grip on her hand.

"It went well… not so much fun because I missed you. I enjoy skiing anyway and wished you had come with me."

Lucy rubbed her hand over his and lifted it to her cheek. "I enjoyed Christmas here in Ivy Creek as well. It reminded me of so many happy memories and helped me decide what I want for the new year."

"Care to share?"

"I'm thinking of expanding," she launched right in. "Business is booming, and even the concession stand has loads of customers during the week. I'm thinking of making the bakery into something bigger. That way, we can make more and host a lot more customers."

Richard was quiet as she spoke, and when she looked at him, his lips were pressed into a thin line that made her pause. "Why do you have that look? Do you not like my idea?" she asked.

"That's not it," he replied. Richard dragged in a deep breath, closed his eyes, and lifted their joined hands so he could kiss her knuckles. His lips lingered for a bit before he continued. "I've tried expanding my business before, and I have to tell you, it's hard. The financial burden becomes a lot at some point, and it will weigh you down. I don't want any of that to happen to you. I like the pace at which you run the bakery right now."

Lucy took in his words and toyed with them in her mind. Expanding the bakery seemed like a brilliant idea to her from the minute she thought about it, but she also hadn't weighed the other aspects Richard just brought up.

She turned to face him again, but she suddenly noticed a queue on the other side of the road. "What's going on there?" she asked, as she observed a few people crossing the road to join the queue.

"Wanna find out?"

Richard was already pulling her across the road with him before she could reply, and they stopped when they made their way past the side of the queue and managed to get into the foyer of the building.

"This place used to be the local theater till it got moved to a new location, and all these people here are..." Richard's voice trailed off when someone walked behind them.

"Are you here for the audition?"

Lucy and Richard both turned to the lady asking.

"Pete Jenson's open auditions for the new play," she continued. "Is that why you're here?"

"There's a new play?" Richard asked the lady.

"Yes," she replied with a smile. "Pete's putting one together, and he intends to take this one around the world. It will be a huge one, judging by the looks of things." She clapped her hands together when she finished, and Lucy noticed the elated look on her face. "So will you be auditioning?"

"No... we're here to watch," Lucy replied, easing her hand away from Richard's so she could tuck her hair behind her ear. "We can watch, right?" she remembered Judy mentioned he was hosting the open auditions, and frankly, Lucy wanted to see for herself what Pete looked like.

She was in luck because the woman standing with them suddenly gasped and looked past them. "That's Pete," she announced, and hurried away before Lucy or Richard could say anything else.

The crowd outside cheered, and Lucy saw Pete wave at some people as he came out from another adjoining door into the foyer. He wore a wide smile as he waved, and she took in his physical looks.

He had a tall, lean figure, and the blue shirt he wore complimented the golden-brown shade of his hair. Pete stopped to listen to what the woman was saying, and as they spoke, she paused and pointed in Lucy's direction.

Lucy's jaw dropped momentarily. Her hand moved to her chest, and she shot Richard a curious look. "I wonder what that's about," she said.

Pete said something to the woman, patting her shoulder as he spoke before he walked away from her with long strides towards Lucy and Richard.

"Pete Jenson," he said when he got to them.

"Lucy Hale," she replied, accepting his hand before Richard mentioned his name.

"Owner of Sweet Delights? That Lucy Hale?" Pete asked, one brow rising with the question.

"Yes, that's me," she answered.

He exhaled and slipped his hands into his pockets. "I've heard so much about you, and your treats, too. I've always wanted to try them as the reviews say you're doing a brilliant job with your recipes. It's good to see young minds creating outstanding products in town."

"Thank you," Lucy replied, flattered that he had a lot to say about her bakery when she had only just met him.

He seems like a nice man, she thought as she assessed him. His eyes were a deep shade of blue and his cheekbones were prominent when he smiled. Lucy could see how he earned a reputation in the entertainment industry. The man had good looks, and there was an easy aura around him.

Two ladies walked past them, and he waved at them, before turning to her and Richard.

"I understand you asked about watching the open auditions. We're yet to start for the day, but there's always room for spectators."

"I'd love to watch, but I have to get back to my bakery," Lucy said, looking at Richard, who nodded in agreement.

"That's sad. You would have enjoyed it. I hope you'll find time to come watch tomorrow. The auditions will last for a week," he said. "By the way, I'd like to contract you to deliver some pastries for the auditions starting from tomorrow. I'd like the production team and main cast to have something to feast on during the rehearsals."

Lucy's insides bounced with excitement at the mention of the offer. Her eyes darted from Pete to Richard before she asked. "That's an amazing offer, and I'd like to take it on. Do you have a list of pastries you'd like to be served? And how about the payment?"

"My secretary will get back to you on both counts as I have to go attend to some business before the auditions start for the day. Don't worry, she'll contact you soon," he said.

Pete gave her one last smile and waved at them before he continued down the hall, entered a room, and closed the door behind him.

"I got an offer," Lucy said, almost letting out an excited squeal as she turned to Richard again. He didn't share in her excitement, and the look on his face dampened her celebratory glow.

"We should go," he said, took her hand and led her out of the foyer again.

Outside, the crowd had reduced because most of the people had entered the theater. Lucy stopped Richard from walking any further and turned to him. She got the sense that he wasn't too excited about her new job offer because it came from Pete.

"This is good news for me, but you don't seem so happy."

Richard faced her. He took out one hand and stroked her chin with it before the lines on his forehead creased. "I am happy for you, Lucy…. The thing is just… you need to be careful when doing business with a man like Pete. Everyone in town knows he's a cunning businessman, and he likes to rip people off. I wouldn't want to see that happen to you."

Her heart swelled with warmth when she saw the look of genuine concern etched onto his face and she sighed.

"I know you worry about me, Richard," she began softly. "But I have a good feeling about this, and I think it will turn out fine," she said. "Trust me on this one."

He shrugged his shoulders. "Just be careful, okay?"

"I promise."

Richard adjusted the lapel of the coat she wore with both hands and pulled her to his side. They continued their walk back down the track they came from. On the way back, Lucy focused her mind on the new job offer, and she tried to think of the possible treats Pete and his secretary might want.

It was the start of the new year, and things were already looking up. With the crowd she saw at the old theater a few minutes ago, Lucy was certain a lot of people would be tasting her treats.

That meant a large order, and good money. She had finally met Pete for herself, and he didn't look like some sleazy man ready to swindle her. If anything, Pete looked professional and she could tell he was adored by many.

What could possibly go wrong with this deal?

She wondered as they arrived at the bakery again.

Nothing.

Lucy answered the dilemma in her head herself as she waved Richard goodbye for the afternoon and entered the bakery to share the good news with her aunt and Hannah. Her new year was truly getting off to a great start.

3

*E*arly the next morning, Lucy hummed to herself as she wrapped the last cupcake and put it in the basket. She glanced at Aunt Tricia, who had just finished making a cup of coffee, and smiled. "Is it ready?"

Aunt Tricia looked up at her from the coffeemaker. "Yes, I just need to add some sugar," she replied. "Are you done packing the treats?"

"Yes, that's all of it for today. Once I get there, I will set up a stand and start selling immediately."

"And how about your payment?" Aunt Tricia asked as she filled a cup. She handed it to Lucy, then filled another for herself. Lucy added cream to hers and tasted it before she sat down to have a sip.

"His secretary contacted me, saying my first payment will come today."

Aunt Tricia paused, and the frown on her face made Lucy smile. "Don't worry about it, Aunt Tricia. I told you I have a good feeling about this," she said.

"Are you sure? I've heard some things about Pete in town myself. People have a lot to say since he started these open auditions, and I don't want him treating you like some of his team."

"Nothing of the sort will happen,' Lucy reassured her aunt before sipping from her cup again.

The door to the bakery swung open and Hannah walked in like a ballet dancer about to put on a performance.

She greeted Aunt Tricia with a hug and rushed to hang her jacket before taking a seat at the table. "The pastries for the sales are ready?"

"Yes," Lucy replied. "I was waiting for you to get here. I'm heading out by ten and before that, I thought we could make a list of the items we need."

"Sure."

Hannah went into the office and returned with a notebook. Lucy started making a list, and she noted down the items until she ran out of what to add.

"I will get them on my way back from the old theater."

"Has Pete paid you for this job yet?" Hannah asked.

Lucy looked from Hannah to Aunt Tricia whose ears had perked up.

"No," she replied, as she noticed a displeased look cross Hannah's face.

"That man does the same thing to everyone. You've got to be careful, Lucy... he might try to rip you off, and not pay for your services."

"Come on... guys," Lucy said, rising to her feet. She kept the optimism in her voice as she continued. "Pete's play is going international, and from the crowd I saw at the theater the other day, there will be a lot of people around for the audition. This is Sweet Delight's chance to go international, too. Try to look on the bright side."

Her positivity didn't rub off on her aunt and Hannah. Both women blinked and stared at her, so she tucked the excessive smile away and dropped her shoulders with a defeated sigh. "All right, I will be wary of Pete Jenson, as you both have advised."

"Good," Aunt Tricia said then and focused on her coffee again. The bakery opened minutes later, and Lucy attended to a few customers before it was time for her to leave.

She ran up to her apartment floor to change her clothes and stood in front of the mirror with her Persian cat, Gigi, sitting at her feet.

"This is a chance for us to get famous, Gigi," Lucy whispered as she played a glamorous scene of her at an international baking talk show being interviewed by some celebrity chef in her head.

Sweet Delights will go international if this goes right... I think this is a good sign.

She smiled again when she bent over to pick Gigi up for a belly rub, then set her on her feet again before picking a brush to ease the strands of her hair.

When she finished applying some makeup, she headed downstairs dressed in a white shirt and black jeans.

A quick drive from her bakery took her to the old theater, and Lucy watched the crowd from her car for a minute. A smile crept up to her face at the thought of everyone complimenting her treats. She had added a new item—waffles, to the list Pete's secretary, Joselyn had asked for, and she knew it would be a hit with anyone who bought it.

Lucy made her way into the theater, and she found Joselyn in the foyer, addressing some men.

"Joselyn," she called with a brilliant smile.

"Lucy… so nice to have you here with your treats. I'm sure everyone will love them already," Joselyn said as she left the people she stood with to meet Lucy. Joselyn was the first woman Lucy met when she first came here with Richard days ago.

"Come with me. There's a stand for you inside the theater, but at the back of the theater," Joselyn said and led Lucy away.

When Lucy arrived at the stand she spoke about, she set her basket on the table and began setting up for the day ahead.

―――

THIRTY MINUTES LATER, Lucy had nearly sold out the waffles she came with. She sat on the chair behind her to rest her legs for a moment but was back on her feet when another man approached the stand.

"One cupcake, please," he said, his head lowered as he placed the order. She handed one to him, and he paid for it before taking a bite. When he raised his head, Lucy saw the dejected look on his face. His eyes were sunk deep into its sockets, and his forehead creased into many frown lines. She didn't ask before he began. "I can't believe I paid a lot of money to get here only to be embarrassed by the famous Pete Jenson."

"What?" Lucy asked. The man raised his head and looked at her.

"I came for the auditions," he continued. "And it was horrible in there. Pete was mannerless, and while I acted out the part he gave to me, he asked me to do some things I found disrespectful. I've been in so much awe of him my entire career, I can't believe he's such a jerk in person. Can you believe he doesn't give anyone a second chance? And he's mean when he tells you off… it's a complete horror show in there."

"I'm so sorry to hear that," Lucy sympathized with him as he finished the cupcake. She saw him scan the other items she had displayed on the table, and he pointed at a doughnut.

"Can I have one of those to-go?"

She nodded her reply and began wrapping the doughnut. Lucy handed it to him and waited for payment. The man stuck his hands into his pockets, but the wallet he pulled out was empty, and it also seemed like he had nothing else left on him when he searched the other pocket and groaned.

Lucy watched him adjust the cuff of his shirt before he looked at her again.

"You can have that one for free," she said, trying to save the man more embarrassment. He already looked mortified, and she didn't want the feeling to increase.

"Thank you," he said. "You're very kind... I wish I hadn't come here; I should have saved myself the embarrassment."

Lucy watched him walk away, then she sighed and ran a hand over her hair. Over the next few minutes, she saw more people walk to the theater. They all wore grim expressions, and it made her wonder how horrible was Pete to these actors?

Lucy remembered her aunt's warning as she lowered herself to her chair again. Was this a terrible idea? She thought, letting self-doubt creep in. Maybe I shouldn't have taken this gig from the start.

4

By mid-day, the queue in front of Lucy's stand had lengthened considerably. Lucy was down to her last waffle, and the other treats were nearly exhausted, too. She served the man in front of her the last waffle and closed the basket.

"We have cupcakes and doughnuts left," she said when the next man in line asked for a waffle. Lucy saw his lips form a tight line before he turned and pulled the last customer before him back.

"You bought the last of the waffles, and you weren't even the next in line," the man said.

"Excuse me?"

Both men faced each other, and the tense expressions they wore made it obvious that the scene would soon turn heated.

"You skipped the line, and now I can't get any waffles because it's gone. It's rude to do that when there are others waiting in line for the same treats you just had."

The man who cut the line poked the other in the chest. "What are you going to do about it?"

He raised his chin and puffed his chest out when the other man shoved him back.

Lucy hurried away from her stand and moved to the scene when hushed murmurs erupted from the rest of the people on the line. She stepped in between both men and raised her arms like a referee warning two opposing players.

"There's no need to argue over the waffles," she began when they pinned their glares on her face. "I'll call my assistant and have her send over more waffles… enough to go round."

Seconds passed before both men parted, walking away in opposite directions, and Lucy exhaled as she took out her phone to place a call to Hannah.

She was excited that people enjoyed her waffles, but she didn't expect that they would fight over it.

"Hannah, good thing you picked up on the first ring. I need you to send more waffles through a dispatch driver to the old theater," she said, looking around to check on the queue of other customers waiting for her to return.

"Sold out the first batch?" Hannah asked from the other end.

"Yes, some men were even fighting over not getting any of the waffles. I confess, I didn't expect to sell out this fast compared to the other pastries I've been selling."

Hannah's breezy laugh tickled her ears.

"I'll send a driver soon, or will you be free to come pick it up?"

Lucy turned to the queue and realized they had already dispersed, some of them walking out of the theater while the others headed towards the rehearsal wing.

"Actually, I'll drop by to get them," she replied quickly before hanging up.

"Everyone, gather around. We're about to start." Joselyn's voice boomed as she came out of the rehearsal wing. She clapped her hands together to gain their attention. "Let's get back on stage, people."

Lucy picked her purse from the table and headed out of the theater. In a few minutes, she had arrived at the bakery. She noticed Hannah was closing the basket she had prepared on the counter.

"How's it going at the auditions?" Hannah asked as Lucy got to the counter. "Is it all glamorous?"

"Not in the least. I had two men fighting over the pastries because one of them cut the line, and it seemed like things would have gotten heated if I didn't step in. Everyone there just wants a shot at being featured in the latest Pete Jenson production, and I get it… they all want a chance to be famous."

"Well, an actor has to suffer for his art," Hannah replied with a shrug.

"Yeah," Lucy murmured before she snatched the basket from the counter and waved at Hannah. "I should get back to the theater."

She was out the door, and in her car again in seconds.

When Lucy arrived at the theater, her stand was empty, so she dropped the basket and headed towards the rehearsal wing.

I can watch the auditions for a bit since I have some time, she thought as she entered.

Inside the auditorium, a lot of the actors were gathered at the front of the stage. She saw Pete address them from where he stood, making dramatic hand gestures as he explained his point.

Lucy stepped closer to the front so she could hear what Pete was saying to everyone.

"When the classical musical comes on, that will be the cue for money to begin to fall from up in the rafters. I need everyone to scramble to get their share of it. Am I clear? I need you all to make this scene believable."

The actors replied in unison, and Pete clapped his hand. When he turned around, her gaze landed on his, and he waved at her, smiling gently before he faced the stage again. He didn't seem too pleased by the way he spoke to the woman beside him. Lucy suspected she was one of his assistants because she nodded and crossed over to the stage to address the actors.

Lucy crossed her hands over her chest as she watched the scene. Pete sat down, and the music came on. The actors in front immediately rushed towards the stage when the cash started raining from above, and their exclamations filled the room.

Although Lucy thought the scene played out perfectly, and the actors looked natural, it didn't seem like it was good enough for Pete because he rose to his feet and stomped towards the stage, waving his hands in the air as he shouted, "Cut!"

The noises continued from the stage. The actors crowded over one another, each of them struggling to get a dollar note from the stacks flying around the stage.

"Cut," Pete shouted.

He dashed towards the scene and tried to get them to stop.

"This is nonsense," he said as the crowd parted for him. "I need you to make it real," he yelled. His voice subdued the clamors coming from the actors.

Lucy crossed her arms over her chest as she watched Pete shove his fingers through his hair and continue. "Let's do it again."

The actors replayed the scene, this time a bit more frantic in their actions, scrambling over each other as they tried to get some of the cash pouring down to the stage.

"Cut," Pete yelled again.

This time, he rushed to the stage. "This is how you do it."

More dollar bills rained down on the stage as Pete joined the actors on the stage. More screams erupted as Pete showed them how, and for a second, Lucy lost track of him in the crowd.

The uproar grew intense this time with people struggling to get some notes dropping to the ground. She saw more people hurry to the stage from the spectators' seats and join in the rabble.

Suddenly a loud piercing scream tore out of the crowd, and slowly everyone dispersed, making room in the center of the stage.

"He's dead," a woman yelled, her tone of voice a hollow sound that sent a chill down Lucy's spine.

Color drained from her face, and she blinked, rooted to one spot as hushed silence filled the auditorium. She spotted Pete Jenson's lifeless body on the floor.

5

Did someone just murder Pete Jenson?

Lucy blinked as she took the left turn leading to her bakery and pressed her foot on the accelerator pedal harder. Her mind still reeled from the shock of what happened at the theater. One minute Pete Jenson was on the stage, directing and voicing his displeasure at the actors' performance, and the next he was lying on the floor, lifeless.

A chill raced through Lucy, and she shuddered from it.

How did this happen?

She tried not to think about it as she continued her drive. If Pete is dead, then the cops will find out about it soon, she told herself. Her mind drifted to the terrified screams of the people on the stage. When the uproar broke, Lucy had hurried out of the auditorium without looking back. The last thing she needed was to get caught up with whatever had happened back there.

Minutes later, Lucy was at her bakery. She slammed the door of her car and dashed into her bakery, holding her purse in one hand, and the full basket of her second batch of treats in the other. Aunt Tricia and Hannah were talking when she entered, and they both turned in her direction.

"How did it go?" Hannah asked, standing to her feet while Aunt Tricia put down the glass of juice she held in her right hand.

"You're back early. I didn't think you'd be back till evening, and why do you still have those?"

Hannah was at Lucy's side as she asked. She took the basket from Lucy, opened it, and peered inside. When Lucy met her gaze again, she saw the question in them.

"Did something happen?" Aunt Tricia asked.

"I… I think Pete Jenson's dead," Lucy announced.

She heard her own heartbeat speed up as she said the words out loud. Hannah's jaw dropped, and out of the corner of her eye, she saw Aunt Tricia push back in her seat and walk to them. The bakery's dining area was empty, so both Hannah and Aunt Tricia steered Lucy towards a chair.

"How? What happened?"

"Pete was trying to get the actors to perform a scene some certain way," Lucy began explaining. "I just got back, and there was no one in the queue at my stand, so I joined the spectators for a bit. Half-way into the scene, and Pete's obviously on edge, complaining that they weren't doing it right. He goes up onto the stage, and shows them how, then there's this loud scream and suddenly people are shuffling away. I only glimpsed Pete lying on the floor. I didn't stay long enough to find out if he was really dead."

Silence filled the dining area when Lucy finished. Her eyes dropped to her hands on her lap, and she licked her dry lips. She replayed the shrill voice that screamed, He's dead in her head, and shut her eyes for a second to get it out of her mind.

"I don't think he's dead," Hannah said suddenly. "Pete's a showman, and he's made his fame from his brilliant productions. It's probably just a stunt to drum up media coverage for his new show."

"You think so, too, Aunt Tricia? Is it possible what happened was just for show?" Lucy asked her aunt, who was still quiet.

"I can't tell. We might have to wait till word gets around."

"I'm not just being skeptical," Hannah continued. "I once watched one of Pete's short plays he performed at some event in Rome on YouTube. In it, he was locked in a cage with lions, and he had to get out alive. A lot of the audience had this stunned expression you have on, but when I watched the making of the video, I realized it was special effects and there were obviously no real lions in that cage.

"Pete's a talented director and actor. You probably witnessed one of his many stunts."

Lucy saw Hannah relax in her chair when she finished speaking, and she moved to join her.

A customer came into the bakery then, and Lucy rose to her feet. She carried the basket of treats into the kitchen, leaving Hannah to attend to the lady and three other customers that walked in.

Inside the kitchen, she unpacked the cupcakes and waffles in the basket, set them on a tray, and returned the basket to the top shelf before letting out a sigh.

Was it possible that scene was a part of some special effects for the production, like Hannah said?

Lucy didn't know what to think. She washed her hands in the sink before carrying the tray of pastries out to the dining area. Hannah and Aunt Tricia worked hand in hand to attend to the customers in the bakery when she returned, and she joined them to assist.

The lady right in front of the counter whispered to the woman by her side as she waited for Hannah to pack her order. "I hear Pete's doing something elaborate for this show he's producing; it has to do with a lot of special effects. I don't know the full story, but a friend of mine is auditioning for the lead role."

"Really?" the second woman replied as their conversation continued.

Lucy shot Hannah a glance as she closed the counter door and took a paper bag from the pile they had to attend to another customer in line.

"I told you it was probably a stunt," Hannah whispered, leaning closer to Lucy as she picked one paper bag for herself.

The women on the line had turned to walk away from the counter, and Hannah moved onto the next customer. "What would you like?" she asked.

They continued to work in rhythmical silence, Lucy pondering on the scene she witnessed, and trying to convince herself that it was just like Hannah had said.

If it's a stunt, then it's a good one because they had me fooled.

They had soon run out of waffles, and Lucy adjusted the apron she wore. "I will go start another mixture for more waffles," she said to Hannah and Aunt Tricia before returning to the kitchen.

Lucy took out a bowl and scooped out some flour. She finished adding the other dry ingredients. She mixed it up while wondering about Pete and his stunts. Could he go to such extreme lengths to add more flare to his production? Maybe that's why he's so famous, she thought.

Lucy knew the ability to go the extra mile could help anyone's career. It certainly helped her when she was in culinary school.

After mixing up the waffles, she set the waffle maker into the oven to pre-heat and set the timer before heading back to the dining area to join Hannah and Aunt Tricia.

She joined them serving, packing up cupcakes and brownies for a man with his wife while Hannah worked on serving some cinnamon rolls and donuts.

Lucy had thought about expanding the area to accommodate more customers, and created more room behind her counter for work, but she had started re-considering the thought after her discussion with Richard.

Lucy wiped her hands on a towel as Hannah turned to her and murmured, a concerned look on her face. "You still worried about what happened at the theater?"

"Yes, it looked like more than a stunt,' she replied. "I mean, you had to hear the terror in the actors' screams as they rushed away from the scene."

"It could be part of the scene," Aunt Tricia commented. "Hannah might be right… you might be worried for no reason. You also said you didn't stick around to see how things developed. So…"

As they conversed, the door opened, and they all turned to see Taylor walk into the bakery. He was dressed in his full uniform, one hand on his waist as he approached the counter. His blonde hair swept away from his face and his jaw was set in a tight line as he stepped over the threshold.

Lucy walked around to greet him first.

"Hi," she began, pasting a smile on her face.

She shook off her anxiety about Pete as she stopped in front of him and pushed her hands deep into the pocket of her jeans. "How are you doing? Are you here for more cupcakes? Or bread?"

Taylor shook his head. She noticed the grim expression on his face as he scanned her bakery before replying. "I'm not here for some treats, Lucy. I'm here on an official assignment."

He faced her squarely, the heat from his blue eyes boring into her face. An inkling that this had to do with Pete filled Lucy's mind even before he said anything else.

"What business?" she asked, her eyes searching his as she tried to maintain her cool, even though her mind was spinning in different directions.

"I'm here to question you about the murder of Pete Jenson."

6

"What?" Lucy asked with a tilt of her head, her voice visibly loud enough to cause heads to stir in the dining area. She drew in a stuttered breath and pressed a hand to her chest, trying to regain composure. Murmurs filled the bakery, and out of the corner of her eye, she saw two customers whisper to each other before glancing in her direction again.

I suspected it, so this shouldn't be that shocking. Still, she struggled with allowing Taylor's words to sink in. Pete was so full of life this morning at the theater, and now he was dead?

"Is everything alright?" one older woman sitting at the far-right end of the bakery asked from where she sat. "Did something happen?"

"Not at all. Lucy just got some good news," Hannah responded before Lucy could speak. Hannah walked around the counter to where the older woman sat and continued speaking to her while Lucy looked at Taylor again.

"Come with me to my office. We can talk privately in there."

She led him into her office, her knees knocking against each other, and shut the door behind them before facing him again. "Pete's dead?" She repeated in a low voice, barely hearing herself, and he simply nodded.

Taylor took off his cap and held it with both hands.

"His body was found on the front stage; he was stabbed, and the paramedics confirmed he was dead when they got to the scene. I understand you were there when it happened, so I came here to get your statement."

Lucy's hand stayed stiff at her sides, and she cleared her throat. "I was there to sell some treats and decided to watch the auditions for a bit. I went into the auditorium, and stood at the back to watch, and Pete was trying to explain a scene to the actors on the stage when suddenly there was a scream. I saw his body on the floor, but I joined the crowd and hurried out before finding out anything else," Lucy said and paused to catch her breath.

"My God, I can't even begin to imagine how this happened," she whispered, looking away from Taylor for a second. When she looked back at him, she saw he was watching her, a furrow between his brows, like he was deep in thought.

"So, what happens next? Am I under investigation because I was at the scene? I was just there to sell my treats as Pete asked me to, and I have no link to any of this," she said, the urge to clear the air filling her even when Taylor hadn't said anything about investigating her.

"Relax, Lucy. I'm just here to get your statement. Nothing else for now."

"For now?" she asked, her brows quirking up.

"Yes, for now. I will be in touch if I need anything else from you because even though we know the cause of death, we know nothing else about the case. You just need to remain watchful till the department figures out what's going on and why Pete was murdered," he advised. "A full investigation will begin, and because of Pete's fame, the town will get a lot of national media descending on the town. This may turn out to be a long investigation for everyone in town."

"Seems like things are about to get interesting around here," she muttered, rubbing a hand on her forehead.

"Yeah... things are about to get very interesting," he repeated. His eyes drifted over her face for a second before he added. "Just do your best to stay out of the spotlight, and don't stir any trouble."

"I won't," Lucy replied almost immediately. She didn't intend to get involved in anything pertaining to Pete's murder.

It's a new year... I've had enough drama in Ivy Creek to last me a lifetime, she thought, remembering the murder investigations she had somehow become entangled in throughout the course of the previous year.

"Good. Take care, Lucy," Taylor said, turning away from her to walk out of the office. She escorted him out to see that the bakery had emptied and waved him goodbye as he walked out the door.

Hannah and Aunt Tricia looked at her with curious stares when they were alone again.

"What did Taylor say?" Aunt Tricia asked, as Lucy lowered herself to a chair and placed her hands on the table in front of her.

"He just confirmed that Pete's dead. I told you it felt like more than a stunt," she said, shifting her attention to Hannah. "He was stabbed right there on the stage."

"Oh my," Hannah muttered. "I heard when he said he came to investigate Pete's death, but I didn't want to believe it was true."

Lucy saw Hannah pale visibly, and her aunt's shoulders sagged.

"I told him I was at the scene, but I got out as soon as the commotion started," Lucy continued. "He said he will be in touch if he needs anything else, and that the investigation would most definitely shake the town."

"That figures," Aunt Tricia muttered. "Pete gained a lot of international attention over the past few years. Many people believed his work was exceptional and a lot of upcoming actors here in town wanted a chance to work with him. It's probably why he came to produce a play here with local actors, years after he gained fame from this same town."

Lucy sighed. Pete's dead. What happens to his show now?

She remembered the pleasant smile he gave her when they had met the first time, and the way he complimented her on her treats. Pete seemed to her like a gentleman, even though she didn't know him much.

So, who would have wanted him dead, and gone through with the plan to murder him?

Lucy couldn't shake the question out of her mind for the rest of the day, no matter how hard she tried.

By the end of the day, Lucy closed the store with Hannah and strolled down the street with her to get some personal items she needed. They crossed the street, and Hannah walked with her into a convenience store.

"It's such a tragedy," Hannah said as they walked down the first aisle. They stopped and Hannah picked up some shower gels. "I was looking forward to what Pete would come up with for this production. I even considered sending in an audition tape."

Lucy looked at her as she picked up a bottle. "Audition? You can act? I thought you didn't think much of Pete Jenson?" she asked.

Hannah shrugged. "I wanted to give it a shot. You never know when lightning will strike. It's such a pity I won't get to find out now."

After tossing a shower gel into her cart, she looked at Hannah again. "Don't worry, I'm sure another opportunity will present itself," she said with a light smile. "As far as I can tell, I think Pete's production has come to a grinding halt. I can't imagine the show going on without him… he had such a captivating aura."

"Yeah, I know," Hannah agreed.

Together, they walked to the front of the store, and as Lucy dropped her items on the counter, the news playing on the TV caught her attention. A female journalist was reporting from somewhere that seemed familiar.

"The murder has left the citizens of Ivy Creek in shock, as Pete Jenson was a pivotal member of their community."

A picture of Pete was displayed on the screen as the reporter continued. It was an image of Pete smiling, his hands raised in a wave.

Who could have done this? She wondered for the hundredth time that day.

"That will be ten dollars and ninety-nine cents please," the attendant said to Lucy, gaining her attention again. She paid with her card and headed out onto the cold streets with Hannah again.

"It's all over the local news, and I'm sure the national one as well," Hannah commented.

"Yes," Lucy replied. She snuggled into the coat she wore and pushed Pete out of her mind. "Good night, Hannah, I will see you in the morning."

"Goodnight."

Lucy watched Hannah cross the street, flag down a cab, and get in before she started down the opposite direction towards her bakery. Once inside, she shut the door and went into her apartment upstairs.

Her cat, Gigi, welcomed her with a purr. Gigi's tail was in an upright position as she waded across the living room with Lucy till she fell onto her couch. Lucy switched on her television and the channel on was the international news station. A huge question mark was displayed on the screen after a short clip of Pete at an award show.

Lucy read the words on the bottom of the screen.

Breaking News - Famous Movie director and actor—Pete Jenson was murdered at a local theater in his hometown.

7

Lucy tied her hair into a bun and swiped her hand down her side.

"Let's say Pete didn't come back to town. Would someone still have murdered him? Or could his killer be someone who's been holding a grudge for years?" she asked, looking at Gigi who sat beside her foot.

She spent the early hours of the morning thinking about Pete's murder and replaying the scene that led to his death in her mind.

His killer must be one of the people on that stage.

Lucy headed into her kitchen to fix Gigi a quick meal before she wrapped a shawl around her neck and headed down the stairs to the bakery. Hannah had sent in a text a few minutes earlier to tell her she wouldn't be around today, so Lucy was looking forward to having Aunt Tricia around to help.

She started the baking early because she was unable to sleep well during the night, and by seven, she turned the door sign to 'open'.

Lucy welcomed her first customer minutes later.

"Good morning, what would you like?" she asked as the man inspected all she had displayed on her counter.

"Three apple pies and a loaf of bread, please," he replied.

"Would you like a coffee to go with that? It's on the house."

The man nodded his head as a smile spread across his face and Lucy proceeded to prepare his order. After him, other customers came in groups, and the next time Lucy got a chance to check her time, it was nearly eleven am.

She took a break since the bakery was empty and took out her cell phone to call Aunt Tricia.

She was supposed to be here hours ago.

Aunt Tricia picked up on the first ring.

"Hey, Lucy, I'm so sorry I couldn't make it there this morning."

"Did something happen?" she asked when she heard the breathlessness in her aunt's voice.

In the background, someone asked, "Can you try to stand on your own, ma'am?"

"It's nothing serious, dear. On my way to the bakery, I tripped on the sidewalk, and I think I hurt my back a little, but I'm all good… you don't have to worry about it. The nice doctor here will patch me up and send me on my way soon."

Lucy frowned. "Oh my God, you should have called me earlier. I'm coming to you now," she said, rising to her feet in a hurry. "Are you badly hurt? You don't have to downplay it, Aunt Tricia. Which hospital are you at? I'm heading there now."

Lucy was already heading for the door when Aunt Tricia protested.

"I'm fine, Lucy. I didn't call because I didn't want you to worry… you're good at that," she said with a tiny laugh.

Lucy didn't believe her aunt was fine, and she would only relax when she saw for herself, so she stepped out of the bakery, turned the sign to 'closed', and locked the door. "Just tell me where you are, Aunt Tricia," she countered, turning her car engine on.

She pulled out onto the road, did a quick reverse, and headed down the road as Aunt Tricia replied. "New Mercy Hospital."

"Great, I'll be with you soon."

She dropped her phone and focused on the road ahead. The sky was clear today even though it snowed the previous day, and Lucy was mulling over her aunt's dilemma. It wasn't uncommon for a woman her age to miss a step, but she worried her aunt took things too lightly.

Lucy remembered once during the holidays; Aunt Tricia nearly slipped in the kitchen. She had blamed it on the shoes she wore, but she was starting to think maybe her aunt wasn't paying attention to the signs her body was telling her she was getting older.

As Lucy drew closer to her destination, she drove past a floristry. The display of flowerpots and the bright yellow color of daffodils displayed in pots caught her attention, reminding her that Aunt Tricia loved the spring flower so much because it reminded her a lot of her childhood in Ivy Creek.

Lucy parked by the store, got out, and walked in to get some flowers for her aunt. She looked around the store when she entered, admiring the botanically designed interior of the shop, and the lush ornamental flowers set aside on the front desk.

"Hi, Lucy," a voice hollered, and Lucy turned to see Judy walk into the store. "I went behind to get some tools, and I noticed the car parked out front. How are you? Are you here to get flowers?"

"Hey, Judy," Lucy greeted. "I didn't know you were a florist," she commented as she smiled at Judy.

Lucy looked at the tiny shovel Judy held, and the gloves in her other hand. Judy wore a brown leather apron over her clothes, her hands were dirty, her cheeks had a smudge, and overall, she looked sweaty, like she had been knee-deep in some work.

"I am," Judy replied. "The shop belonged to my mother, and I love the life flowers give, so I kept it when the chance came. It's just like you did with your mother's bakery. I love what you've done with Sweet Delights."

"Thanks, Judy," Lucy said, admiring Judy's charm and kind words. "I would like a bouquet, please," Lucy said, getting to the business of why she had stopped by. For a second, she wondered if Judy would bring up something about Pete's death.

Everyone in town was talking about it. She wondered if Judy knew Pete well or if their relationship had strictly been work based.

She ought to wonder what happened too.

Judy had walked over to the counter where her pots were displayed, and she waved a hand at them as she pinned her eyes on Lucy's. "All right, what kind do you intend getting? Have anything specific in mind?"

Lucy paused and looked around the collection on the table in front of her. She touched one petal of a lily, and looked at Judy again, meeting the woman's blue eyes. "Something that depicts healing."

"I think a bouquet of lavender is what you're looking for," Judy replied, pointing at an already prepared bouquet. "As you know, the scent is therapeutic, and the color is just so lovely."

Lucy agreed with her. "I'll take it."

She watched Judy gather her a bouquet, and she looked around the store one more time. The setting was like something Lucy envisioned for an upgrade to her bakery. A larger setting, with space for more tables, and larger, rectangular windows to let in more light."

"Thank you," Lucy said as she took the bouquet from Judy and reached into her coat's pocket for her wallet. "I really love your shop, Judy. Pleasant setting, and very spacious," she commented, but stopped mid-way when she realized she didn't have her wallet.

I must have left it in my apartment in a rush to get to Aunt Tricia, she thought, chiding herself internally at her forgetfulness.

"I know... I started out small with very few customers, but with a commitment to excellence and improving, I now have a steady flow of customers, even from the big cities, who trust my judgment, and always patronize me."

"That's so lovely." Lucy smiled again and rubbed her eyebrow. "Judy... I kind of left my wallet at home in my rush to get out," she said, stretching her hands out to return the flowers. "I don't think I'll be able to get these."

"Oh, no, no, don't worry about that, Lucy. You can drop by to pay me later," she said, pushing Lucy's hands back. "I insist."

"Thanks for this, Judy," she replied. "And for the contract to deliver treats to the town's council meeting."

Judy waved her hand and let out a short laugh. "That was nothing... you're doing a good job of keeping up your parents' legacy and I like that. You just need to always think of growing because if you're not, then you're dying. Business wise, of course," she added after a second of silence and chuckled again.

"Thanks, Judy. I'll drop by to pay for these later today," Lucy thanked her again as she waved goodbye.

She got to the door and pushed it open when Judy said in a light tone behind her. "Have a nice day, and I wish whoever gets the flowers a quick recovery."

As Lucy came out to the front porch, she had to quickly side-step to let a woman enter the flower shop. Lucy's head snapped to the side as the woman passed her. She caught the familiar scent of a perfume.

Where have I seen that face?

Lucy contemplated for a second before continuing to her car. Through the large windows, she saw Judy smile at the woman inside the store and laugh at something they said to each other.

She looks familiar, she thought again as she set the flowers on the passenger seat and continued her journey.

8

Lucy found her aunt at the out-patient unit after inquiring at the nurse's station. Aunt Tricia sat upright on the hospital bed, her hands in front of her, as she listened to what the doctor standing by her bedside was saying.

Her body sagged with relief when she saw a smile on Aunt Tricia's face, and most of her worry ebbed away. Even in a hospital gown, Aunt Tricia seemed at ease, her hands crossed on her lap as she wriggled her ankles on the bed.

Thank goodness, she's actually alright.

"Hi," Lucy breathed out as she got to the bed and hugged her aunt briefly before handing over the flowers she held. "How is she?" she asked the doctor as Aunt Tricia took the flowers from her and inhaled them deeply.

"Lavender… I love them, thanks Lulu, they're really lovely…" she said with a tiny smile that Lucy returned as she watched her inhale the scent of the flowers again.

Lucy placed her hand on her aunt's shoulder, waiting for the doctor's reply.

"Everything looks fine, and she's lucky she didn't break anything from her fall," the doctor replied. "We will keep her for a few days for more observation, and you can come for her on Friday," he added.

"Friday?" Aunt Tricia protested. "That's three days away… can't I go sooner?"

"No madam," the doctor replied, then left them after giving Lucy a brief nod.

Alone with her aunt, Lucy dragged in a deep breath, and turned to her. "You need to be more careful, aunt," she cautioned. "That fall could have gone badly in many ways, and I don't think I can stand you getting hurt."

"I'm fine, Lucy," Aunt Tricia replied, and took her hand. "Now don't ruin your lovely face with that ugly frown, dear. I put on some weight during the holidays and it's affecting my balance. It's nothing too serious, so you shouldn't worry."

Lucy sat on the chair near the bed and put her hands in front of her. "You should be more careful," she said before putting her hands into the pocket of her coat.

"I will, I promise," Aunt Tricia replied. "Did you lock up the bakery to come see me?"

She answered with a nod and relaxed into the chair. "I rushed out, just turned the sign to closed because I had to make sure you're fine."

"Thanks, dear, but you really should get back to the bakery. It's lunch hour at this time, and you'll miss a lot of customers if you stay."

Aunt Tricia had a point, and even though Lucy was reluctant to leave because she just got there, she still rose to her feet.

"I'll come check on you in the evening," she said, and kissed her aunt on the cheek. "Try not to fall off the bed this time."

Aunt Tricia chuckled. "All right, dear."

On the drive back home, Lucy noticed an older woman strolling down the sidewalk with the help of a younger lady. The picture of them both together brought back her anxiety about Aunt Tricia.

Her aunt wasn't getting younger, and it was growing obvious that she needed more help and assistance in getting around.

Living alone probably isn't ideal, she thought as she took the bend leading to the bakery. While Aunt Tricia lived on her side of town, she was still not close enough for Lucy to check up on her as much as she'd like.

Would having her move in with me be a good idea?

The second the thought entered her mind, she deliberated on it. Having Aunt Tricia closer to her was a better option for both. That way, Lucy could keep an eye on her while still going about her business.

The only issue was her apartment above the bakery would be cramped to accommodate them both. She drove past the town's local church and continued down the road, speeding past the turn leading to the high street without even realizing it.

She drove past her intended turn, and when she realized, she stopped and did a U-turn to get back on track. Lucy was familiar with this street as it was where she grew up. Her parents' house stood by the left side towards the end of the road, and when she got to it, she parked by the curb and got out.

With quick strides, she got to the front of the picket fence separating their house from the main road and propped her hands on her waist.

It feels like I haven't been here in years when it was only just last year that they passed away.

As she stood there in front of the house, a memory flashed in her head, one of her riding her bicycle around the yard, and her mother shouting for her to be careful from the porch where her father worked on a broken stair.

"I'll be careful, mommy," Lucy remembered her reply like it happened just yesterday. A short laugh escaped her lips as tears filled her eyes. Seconds after she promised to be careful, she fell from the bike, and her mother had dashed to her side immediately.

More fond memories rushed through her, creating a swirl of emotions Lucy hadn't felt in a while. Her lung clenched for a second, and when she released the breath she held, it came out in a whoosh. There was a cold bite to the air that stung her ears. Even though the day started out warmer, the weather was gradually changing.

Settling her shaky insides, Lucy walked past the lawn to the front porch. She reached under the flowerpot at the far end of the wooden, narrow porch and grabbed the keys she kept hidden there.

She entered the house, taking her time to walk around the living room. The place looked the same, except it was covered in dust, and cobwebs swamped the corners of the celling boards.

This place is big enough to house Aunt Tricia and me.

Lucy hadn't once thought of selling her parents' house even though she also hadn't considered moving in. It was the first time since she had arrived back in town that she had considered moving in.

Her phone rang in her pocket, pulling her out of her thoughts. "Hey, Hannah," she said when she picked up on the second ring.

"Hi, Lucy… I stopped by the bakery on my way back from my outing with my sister, and you aren't here. What's happening? We just drove off now, but I had to call to check in."

"I'm on my way back," she replied. "Had to check in on Aunt Tricia. She had a nasty fall earlier this morning, and she's in the hospital."

"Oh, my God! Is she all right?"

"Yes, yes, she's fine—she insists I shouldn't worry, but you know how I get. I just had to make sure she was all right. I'm driving back to the bakery now; I'll be there in a few minutes."

When she dropped the call, Lucy's eyes swept around the kitchen where she stood. She walked out, locked the door behind her, and this time, slipped the key into her pocket.

I'm moving back in, she told herself as she got into her car and turned on the engine. It was time to act on the urge she had to do something different this year. Expanding the bakery had been her first option, and she planned on moving on with it.

As Lucy drove away, she stared at her reflection in the center mirror of her car. Judy's words played in her mind. If you're not growing, you're dying.

"I can do this," she said to herself. The expansion of the bakery would take a while, and she would move back to her parents' house before starting.

That way, she could be with Aunt Tricia, monitoring her while the work went on. It was a brilliant idea, and Lucy knew the first thing she had to start with was changing the narrative of how she thought of the house.

From now on, it was her house... not just her parents'. Lucy stepped on the accelerator pedal to speed up so she could get to the bakery faster. It was lunch hour, like Aunt Tricia said, and she had to get back to work.

9

Lucy and Hannah finished cleaning the next morning after baking. It was quite early, and the first stream of customers for the day just left the dining area when Lucy faced Hannah. "I've decided to expand the bakery. It took me a while to be convinced about it, but yesterday, after the incident with Aunt Tricia, I finally decided."

"It's an excellent decision, Lucy," Hannah said.

"Thanks," Lucy replied as she opened the display glass to pick a cupcake. She nodded as she bit into it. "Yes, it will give this place a fresh look for the year, and also allow the customers more space to enjoy their treats."

Hannah was wiping the counter with a napkin as she turned to Lucy again.

"It also gives us more preparation room. If we can make the kitchen bigger, the table and shelves can be expanded as well. Speaking of shelves, that reminds me, we've run out of syrup and whipped cream."

"I'll get them today," Lucy replied.

They continued their conversation for a while, Lucy going over the plans she had already formed in her head concerning the expansion.

"If the counter comes forward a bit, then we can even make a stairway leading up to another dining area. It will be cozier up there, and customers who sit there will have a good view of the high street and the mountains in the distance."

"So that means you'll be moving out?" Hannah asked.

Lucy cast a glance over at her as she counted the cupcakes left. She saw Hannah's hands come over her chest as she leaned against the counter.

"Yes, I'll move back to my parents' house," she replied, then remembered her new narrative. "I'll move back to my house," she corrected with a smile. "With Aunt Tricia, I'm thinking of keeping a keen eye on her, really for my peace of mind."

"That's a good idea," Hannah agreed. "I think you moving in there will be great. Besides, it shows you're actually planting roots here."

The door opened, and a customer walked in wearing a cheery smile. "Hello… Happy new year," she greeted as she got to the counter. "I'd like some waffles, please. I had them yesterday, and I can't stop remembering how wonderful they tasted, especially the ones with the sliced berries."

"Coming right up," Lucy replied.

She immediately started packing the order while whistling to herself, and when she was done, she handed the paper bag to the lady. "Here you go. That will be three dollars."

The lady reached into the pocket of her coat. Her eyes widened suddenly as her hands flew to her mouth. "Oh shoot, I think I left my wallet at home. Oh God, I was in such a hurry to get to work, I didn't even realize—I'm so sorry," she babbled.

Lucy blinked. She smacked a hand on her forehead, her mind jumping to the previous day when she promised to return to Judy's store. "Oh no," she exclaimed.

"Please don't be mad. I truly didn't know," the lady whispered again.

"It's fine, really. I'm not mad," Lucy answered. "You actually just did me a favor, reminding me of something I have to do real quick. I have to go now, but you can have the waffles for free," she continued, giving her a sidewards glance as she rounded the counter, dashed for her coat hanging in the office, checked it for her wallet and keys before heading out of the bakery.

When Lucy arrived at Judy's store a few minutes later, Judy was standing on the patio. Judy welcomed her with a wide smile.

"I'm really sorry, Judy. I promised to come back yesterday, but I skipped on that. It genuinely escaped my mind, and it just came to me, so I had to rush here."

"It's nothing, Lucy. I trust you… I knew you would come eventually," she said.

"Thank you," Lucy replied. She reached into her coat for her wallet. "How much did the flowers cost?"

"Thirty dollars," Judy replied. "Come in, I should write you a receipt for that."

Lucy rubbed a hand on her chest as she inhaled the crisp air deeply, filling her lungs with it. Inside the store, she looked around again, admiring the wooden stands where Judy displayed her flowers.

"Here you go," Judy said when she returned from the table, where she wrote a receipt. "Thanks for coming back."

"I should be thanking you," Lucy replied as Judy took the cash. "My aunt really loved the flowers."

"You can come back anytime if you want more. Maybe something to brighten up your bakery or house. Flowers are nice aesthetics, and they brighten up the mood."

"You're right, maybe I should look around," Lucy agreed.

She followed Judy around, checking the vases of lilies and pansies. When she reached the last stand, she noticed a newspaper lying on it.

Lucy's heart somersaulted when she saw the picture of Pete Jenson. She scanned the headline on the front page before facing Judy again.

"It's a tragedy what happened to Pete," Judy said, starting the conversation about Pete. "Even though he had many flaws, he didn't deserve to go down like that."

"Flaws?" Lucy repeated. She slipped her hands into her coat pocket and gauged Judy's expression as she talked.

Judy's brittle smile showed again when she answered. "Yes, flaws. Whenever he was in town, he threw his weight around, stepping on toes and leaving a cloud of strife and anger. But it all goes away once he leaves town. All he does is talk bad about the town when he's away."

"I see," Lucy murmured the words, as she chewed on her thoughts. "But who would have killed him?"

"Probably someone he must have offended," Judy replied with a shrug. "Someone who can't get over what he did to them."

Lucy was about to comment when the door opened, and a lady walked into the store. Lucy recognized her from the last time she was there. The woman had striking looks. Long blonde hair that fell to her waist in straight strands, and delicate facial features.

Lucy noticed the poise of her body as she walked into the store, and her gaze lingered as the lady took off her coat, looked in their direction for a second, but made her way into the back of the shop without saying anything to them.

Lucy cocked her head to one side and rubbed a finger over her lower lip.

I'm sure I've seen her somewhere, Lucy contemplated, trying to figure out the face. "I have seen her before," she mumbled.

"Seen who?" Judy asked.

Lucy looked up at Judy and sighed. "It's just… the lady who walked in looks really familiar. I'm certain I've seen her before," she replied.

"Oh… that was Thelma," Judy replied, her lips curving. "She's my daughter."

"Oh…"

"You probably know her because she starred in a toothpaste commercial when she was younger. Thelma gained a lot of attention after that commercial."

Judy struck a pose then and went ahead to act out the commercial.

"Want a brilliant smile?" she said at the end, propped both hands on her hips, and widened her grin just like it was acted in the commercial.

Lucy chuckled, recalling the commercial as she watched Judy act it out. "I remember when that commercial first aired. I loved it so much and always admired the girl's lovely smile," she teased, laughing as Judy straightened.

"You're good at acting yourself. The way you just played that out, it was like I was watching the commercial all over again," Lucy said with a hearty chortle. "I just wondered because it also seems like I've seen her recently."

"You probably have," Judy replied as Lucy started walking towards the door. "She's an actress, and she was in Pete's production."

10

Lucy stopped by the grocery store on her way back to the bakery. She checked her watch after pulling into a parking spot and hurried into the store to grab the items Hannah mentioned earlier.

"Syrup, and whipped cream," she muttered to herself as she got to the baking aisle and searched for the products she enjoyed using. She picked them up, and walked towards the counter, but stopped when her eyes caught the papers hanging on a rack.

Lucy looked and shoved her fingers through her hair. She wondered when his death would be old news.

Two men stood in front of it, their hands inside their pockets. She moved closer to see Pete's picture on every front page. Lucy shook her head.

"I think he deserves what he got if you ask me," one man said to the other as they stood in front of the newspaper rack.

"Don't say that... it's bad enough that Pete came back to town when no one really wanted him around. Now, his face is plastered on every newspaper, and there will be a lot of useless publicity this town doesn't need," the other replied. "I didn't like Pete either, but I feel he should have died elsewhere."

Lucy stood beside them quietly, reading the headlines on the newspapers as she held her cart.

"What do you think about it?" the taller man asked, turning to face her. "Don't you also think that his death has caused a nuisance in town?"

Lucy shook her head. "I don't think it's my business," she replied, meeting their gaze. The shocked look on the men's faces satisfied her as she walked over to the counter to pay for her items.

Some people need to gossip less, she thought to herself as she got to her car and drove off.

Lucy walked into her bakery to find Hannah serving customers at the counter. Some women seated at a table were also talking about Pete's death in hushed tones.

"How were things while I was gone?" Lucy asked as she fell into rhythm with Hannah behind the counter. She handed prepared orders to the customers while Hannah took more orders.

"I don't want to be insensitive, but I'd like to turn off the news for a bit," she commented when they served the last one in the short queue and had some time to themselves.

"Pete's death is all anyone's talking about."

Both Lucy and Hannah stole a look at the table where the women talked in audible tones about what happened at the theater. She remembered the scene vividly but tried not to relive it.

"I was right there when it happened, and I think it must be one of the actors… it had to be one of them," a lady at the table said.

"It's best we don't get involved," Hannah replied, drumming her fingers on the countertop. "We have a good thing going on here and getting involved in this murder case might ruin it."

Lucy didn't need to be reminded what could happen when she meddled with anything that didn't concern her. When she moved back to Ivy Creek, a murder was committed on her property, and it affected her business in every way. She couldn't let that happen again.

"You're right," she said, and exhaled. Lucy looked around the bakery to see it had emptied, so she reached for the remote under the counter and turned off the TV.

"Today, I met the young girl from the famous Crest 3D white commercial," Lucy began. She put her hands on her waist, struck a pose, and mimicked the commercial. "Want a brilliant smile?"

Hannah chuckled, covering her mouth with her right hand as she laughed out loud. "I remember that advert, and also the girl… what was her name again?"

"Thelma," Lucy replied.

"Yes, Thelma. She was in my year in high school, and we finished together. She was always so full of herself because of the popularity of that ad."

"Well, I met her today. More like glimpsed her actually… she's Judy Cousins' daughter, the woman we met at the town's council meeting the other day."

"Really? I didn't know that."

Lucy and Hannah moved to the front porch to relax a little with a glass of water.

Hannah voiced her opinions on the expansion plans, and Lucy went over it with her, vividly imagining what the new bakery would look like, and trying to figure out how they could work on this project without affecting sales at the bakery.

Lucy waved her hand to the end of the narrow porch where they sat. "We can make the porch wider a bit since we're adjusting things. It will give more room for the dining area downstairs, and the stair that will be constructed."

"I think it's a good idea to re-paint the wood and give the place a total make-over… more vibrant colors."

Lucy experimented with that idea in her head. "What of pastel shades?" she asked.

"Sounds terrific," Hannah beamed, clapping her hands together.

Lucy's insides rumbled with her building excitement. The building would look better overall if she went along with this plan, and she could almost see how the improved look would attract more customers and improve her bank balance.

Relaxing in her chair, she looked at the lawn out front, and back at Hannah. "I will need to work with a professional, someone with more in-depth knowledge on renovations and interior designs because I want to give this my best."

Her heart swelled at the thought of starting something new.

This is the kind of energy I need this new year… more things to get me pumped up for the months ahead.

"I have an uncle who's in that field," Hannah responded immediately. "His name is Keith, and he runs an interior design firm here in Ivy Creek. He's the finest interior designer in town as far as I'm concerned." Hannah paused, took out her phone from her pocket and began showing her some pictures. "Here, let me show you some of his work," Hannah continued.

"He worked on our house recently, totally transforming our fireplace and the kitchen. My mom fell in love with the wall designs immediately."

"I also love them," Lucy agreed. "I think you should ring him up," she said.

She waited, watchful of Hannah's facial expressions as she dialed the number. Lucy saw her eyes suddenly light up.

"Hey, Uncle Keith, how are you? I'm great, too. Are you in town? I have a friend here who needs an interior designer, and she's looking to book an appointment."

Lucy kept her focus on Hannah as the conversation played out.

"Right, thanks so much. I'll let her know."

When Hannah dropped the call, she said, "He says he's around, and we can come check on him today or tomorrow if we'd like. I can go with you, or give you directions, whichever you'd prefer."

"There's no rush at the bakery today," Lucy said as she looked around. "We can go now… I'd like to go now."

She couldn't hide her excitement, and most of all, her instincts told her this was the right time to push forward. "I'm too excited to wait, actually," she added as she rose to her feet.

Hannah followed her inside, and they headed back out together after checking around the kitchen to make sure they hadn't forgotten to turn off anything.

Lucy turned on the radio as they drove down the road, and she changed the station when the first thing she heard was a report on Pete's death.

I don't want anything spoiling my mood right now; she thought as she tuned in to a music station. Hannah knew the lyrics to the R n B song playing, so they sang along as she followed Hannah's directions to their destination.

"I so loved this song growing up," she commented, grinning as she tapped the steering wheel while keeping her attention on the curvy road ahead of them.

Lucy had a good feeling about the plans she had set in motion.

Everything will turn out all right. I just can't wait to see what designs Hannah's uncle will have to suggest to me.

11

"Keith Meyer," the man said when Lucy walked into the office with Hannah. "Nice to meet you."

"Lucy Hale. Likewise," she replied, and took the seat he offered. "Hannah said a lot about your designs, and I couldn't wait to see them."

"I've also heard a lot about your bakery, and I've tasted a few of your pastries. They are absolutely the best. I knew your parents, God bless their souls, and I think you're doing a good job keeping the family business alive."

"Thank you, Mr. Meyer."

"Please, it's Keith."

She saw him smile at Hannah.

"How are you, Hannah? It's been a while since I dropped by at the house. How are your parents?" he said.

"Everyone's great," Hannah replied.

Keith took a seat at his side of the table, and Lucy joined him after taking off her apron.

"You should have a look at my catalogue," he said, reaching into the drawer by his side.

Lucy took the catalogue from him as he said, "I have these designs for businesses like yours, and I think one of these should work well with the structure of your bakery," he continued, pointing at the picture on the catalogue she was viewing.

Lucy met his gaze, and he added. "I've been inside the bakery once. I think I remember what it looks like in the dining area, but I will need to take another look."

"What do you think about these floor patterns?" Lucy asked Hannah. They went over the designs and the size of the expansion they were looking at. Lucy wasn't sure what she wanted yet, but she knew something subtle and yet different would suffice.

"Would you mind if I took a few days to mull over this? Everything I see here is great, and I'd like to decide."

Keith grinned. "Sure, you can do that. I will email you a brochure, so you can ponder on the designs there until you make a choice."

"I appreciate that."

She scribbled her email on a piece of paper he offered, and he gave her his business card in exchange.

When Lucy and Hannah stepped out of the firm, they stood by the car for a second. "His designs looked really lovely… I think I liked the ones with the white tabletop joined to the display glass by the side, and the lights dropping from the ceiling."

"Me too... that one really gives off a cozy vibe with the spaciousness. There are shelves on the wall too and you can display bread and some other pastries there. The seats in front of the counter also give the customers a chance to seat while waiting for their order."

"I might decide on that one," Lucy said. "I'll just give it some time."

She glanced at her watch and looked across the road. Richard's café was just a few blocks away from there, and she considered giving him a surprise visit.

"Do you mind going back to the bakery alone?" she asked Hannah. "I'd like to check on Richard."

A flicker of a mischievous smile crossed Hannah's lips. "You should have packed him a tiny basket," she suggested. "It's always fun to have surprise visits with a present at hand."

Hannah winked at her and shook her head as she walked to the side of the road. "It's all right. I'll head back to the bakery."

Lucy waited till Hannah got in a cab before she drove and parked at Richard's café. When she entered, Richard was scribbling a name over a plastic cup, and the wide grin on his face immediately made Lucy smile.

He paused for a second when he saw her but recovered from his surprise as she got to the counter. The ladies he served hurried away, giggling amongst themselves as they exited the cafeteria.

"Caramel latte for me with soy milk, please," she said in a light tone.

Richard winked at her. He put his hand over hers on the counter briefly before he replied. "Coming right up. Soy milk is nice and if you don't mind, I'd like to sit with you and have some."

"Are you always this charming with the customers?" she asked, laughing as he handed her a cup, then walked around the counter to meet her.

Lucy took a seat, sipped from the cup, and waited till Richard took off his apron and joined her.

"It seems to drive the customers in," he said. "It's a strategy. People feel comfortable in places where they are treated with care, and I try my best to do that."

He stopped for a second, his hand drawing circles on hers on the table. "Are you in the neighborhood for something? Or was this just a surprise visit? If it's the latter, then I'm really loving that you came. We can spend some time together this evening if you aren't busy."

"This is a surprise visit, but I was around here to see someone."

When he quirked a brow, she continued. "Keith Meyer, the owner of the interior designs firm. I'm thinking of moving through with the expansion of the bakery and moving back into my home."

"Your family house?" he asked.

She nodded. "It's mine, and there's no reason to run from it. I think this is a good thing, the expansion… moving back into my house… it's a sign that I'm growing."

Lucy expected a different reaction from Richard. Maybe his usual charming smile and witty words, or some enthusiasm, but he stared at her blankly for a second before withdrawing his hand.

"You moved forward with the expansion anyway," he said, and pushed back on his chair to rise to his feet.

Lucy stood up after him. Her cup of latte lay forgotten as she followed him, closing the distance between them.

She put a hand on his arm and stopped him from walking any further. "Why do I sense that you're not in the least bit excited for me?"

When Richard simply shrugged, picked up a napkin, and began wiping a table, she scoffed. "I can't believe this… you should be happy for me. What is the problem?"

"It's not like I'm not happy for you, Lucy. I am, but…" his voice trailed off, and he shoved his fingers through his hair. "Why do you have to expand? It's a hassle, and you'd spend a lot. Why not keep running things smoothly as you are now? Even though it's small?"

His words echoed through her, sucking wind out of her lungs like she was punched in the face. She licked her lips once and rubbed her forehead.

Richard looked at her again. "I'm sorry, it's just I don't get why you need to grow bigger."

"I get it," she answered, and pushed the strands of hair falling to the side of her face away.

Richard's eyes drifted over her again before the door opened and some students walked right past her to the counter.

He was instantly his usual charming self again as he attended to them, and Lucy turned to get back to her seat. She lifted her cup to her lips again, but the latte had gone cold, and she had lost the urge to enjoy it.

Why isn't he supportive of my decision? He should be happy for me... this is a good decision. I don't get him.

She stole a glance at him again and exhaled deeply. There's definitely a reason why he is being this way.

With a sigh, she dropped the cup and got up to walk out of the cafeteria. Just then, the door opened, and a man walked in. He looked over his shoulder as he closed the door behind him, wiping the sweat beading on his forehead with the sleeve of his coat. His hands shook visibly as he dropped them to his side and adjusted his coat.

Lucy recognized him as one of the men fighting at her stand at the theater the day Pete was murdered. Her pulse skipped a beat as he drew closer, but walked right past her like he hadn't seen her.

I don't think he recognizes me.

"Hello, what would you like to have?" she heard Richard ask when he got to the counter. Lucy put her hands deep into her pocket and contemplated confronting him for a second.

Richard was smiling when she looked back, and she saw the man take the plastic cup Richard offered, exchanging it for some cash.

Lucy sucked in a deep breath, and without re-thinking her choice, she stepped forward to have a chat with him.

Who knows, he might know something useful about the ongoing investigation.

12

Lucy tapped the man on his shoulder once, and he spun around. His eyes widened when they landed on hers, and his coffee spilled a little from the plastic cup he held.

"Holy moly, you scared me!" he exclaimed, eyeing her.

"I'm sorry, I didn't mean to," Lucy apologized. "Do you mind having a little chat? There are some things I'd like to ask you."

The man looked over his shoulder at the counter where Richard was now attending to a customer, and Lucy adjusted her coat as she waited for his reply. He pretended to cough, then followed her to a corner of the café where they sat facing each other.

Lucy took a second to take in the man's physical looks. He had straw-blond hair and looked like he had just gotten a tan. His lips parted as he took a sip from his cup, and Lucy noticed his wiry fingers.

"I'm Lucy Hale," she said. "We met at the theater on the day of…" she stopped as she was about to say Pete's murder. "On the day of the open auditions," she said instead.

The man nodded. "Freddie Burrow. I remember you from the theater. You're the lady who sold the treats that day," he replied, proving to Lucy that he remembered her, too. "And it's all right to say Pete's murder. I admit it bothers me when I think about it, but I'm trying to be more comfortable accepting what happened."

He dragged in a deep breath when he finished talking and took a sip from his cup.

"Why does it bother you?" Lucy asked, gauging his expression.

"Pete was a tough boss. I performed in some of his productions when he lived in Ivy Creek, and when he came back, I was one of the first people he reached out to. He was a perfectionist, I knew him well, but… what happened that day shocked everyone. The cops have questioned me a few times about it, and I still can't get comfortable enough with the way everyone looks at me when I'm in public."

As he talked, Lucy noticed a few people glance in their direction.

"What did the cops ask you about?" she questioned, focusing on him again. "Do you know if they've found out anything about the murder?"

Freddie shook his head. "They asked a few questions about what happened before the murder. Where Pete had been, and who he'd been with. I told them all I knew. The scene we were rehearsing was already perfect, but it's in Pete's nature to make it exceptional, so he pushed harder. He wanted it to be more frantic because he believed that would make it better. I told the police this, and that I had nothing to do with his death. They asked me not to leave town till the end of the investigation."

"I see." Lucy twisted a button on her jacket as she watched him.

Freddie adjusted himself on his chair and emptied his cup before standing up. "I need to go… I'm sorry for the commotion I caused at your stand that day. I wasn't my best self that day."

"It's alright, it happens to the best of us," she replied.

Freddie gave her one last look before he turned and walked out of the café.

Sitting alone, Lucy looked at Richard again. She realized she was waiting for him to come over so they could continue their conversation, but Richard hadn't looked in her direction the entire time she sat there with Freddie.

She rubbed her forehead and rose to her feet to get out of the store. Lucy checked her watch as she drove off from the store and dropped by the hospital to check on Aunt Tricia. When she walked into the ward, her aunt was being her usual charming self with the nurses, and she was rolling around the corridor in a wheelchair.

"How are you feeling?" Lucy asked when she got to her. She put a hand on her aunt's shoulder and massaged it gently.

"I'm great, Lucy. I can even stand and walk properly on my own."

They began making their way to her aunt's ward. When she got to the ward, she helped her up from the wheelchair.

"What's happening at the store?" she asked. "I feel like I've missed out on a lot."

"You've not missed out on much," Lucy said and sat beside her on the bed. "I'm thinking of expanding the bakery, and that means I will move back into the house on Easton Street. I want you to come with me. That way, I can monitor you and make sure you don't have another incident."

"You worry too much," Aunt Tricia said with a laugh.

They spent some time together; Lucy went over the details of the idea she got from Keith Meyer, and she showed her the brochure Keith emailed to her.

"I love this one," Aunt Tricia said, pointing at a picture.

"Me too… It was one of my favorites." She returned her phone to her coat pocket and sighed.

"But you don't look so happy though," Aunt Tricia continued.

"It's just…" Lucy rubbed the back of her neck to ease some of the tension there, but it still ebbed through her veins slowly. "I told Richard about the expansion, and even though I was so excited, he didn't feel the same way. He practically told me to continue being small, that he likes me that way."

"Nonsense, dear," Aunt Tricia responded immediately. "He obviously didn't mean that."

Lucy replayed the conversation she had with Richard, and the way he dismissed her after that, acting like she wasn't still in his café as he attended to his customers. "No… I think he really wasn't pleased to hear I'm expanding. He also didn't hesitate to show his disapproval." She fell silent for a second, then added with a shrug. "Not that his approval will make me change my mind. I just thought he would at least be happy for me and show some support."

"You will get all the support you need from Hannah and me, all right?"

Lucy chuckled when Aunt Tricia reached out to stroke her hair. Her aunt was the confidence boost she had needed, and hearing her words of encouragement was enough to push Lucy on.

"I should get back to the bakery and help Hannah out," she said, rising to her feet again. "You'll be out of here soon, and hopefully the house will be ready by then."

"Take care," Aunt Tricia said.

Lucy waved at her one last time before she exited the ward. As she walked to her car in the parking lot, she noticed a flier stuck to her windscreen.

Lucy looked around to see if anyone sharing fliers was hovering around. When she found no one, she picked up the flier and read it.

Audition for a role in the latest Pete Jenson production.

Lucy stared at it for a long time. She wondered what would happen at the theater in Pete's absence. She had expected the production would stop, or maybe pause until the investigation was over.

Who would distribute these leaflets even though Pete's dead?

A wild thought flew in her head just then as she rumpled the paper in her hand. What if the secret to Pete's murder lies at the theater?

She scratched an itch on her nose and got in her car. Lucy drove by the theater to see what was going on there for herself.

I might find a clue if I look closely, I'm almost certain of it.

13

It was nearly three pm as she headed for the theater. The road seemed unusually busy as Lucy drove past a few diners and stores before taking the turn leading past the station.

She noticed a crowd of reporters gathered in front of the station, taking pictures, and clamoring for a chance to ask their questions.

She focused ahead again when she passed the station, and minutes later, she was pulling up in front of the local theater. Lucy got down from her car, walked towards the entrance, and paused as a frown spread across her face. She expected to see a crowd gathered around her for the ongoing auditions, or maybe more people inside, but the place looked deserted.

With careful steps, she neared the door, pushed it open, and entered. Inside, the theater was empty too, no sign of a soul hovering around.

Maybe the flier I saw was an old one?

There was slow music coming from inside the rehearsal wing, and as Lucy stood there, she considered checking if anyone was in there. The music played slowly, the instrumental tone filling the air. Its sound reminded her of the ominous scene Pete had been trying to pull off on the day of his death.

Stilling the sudden rumble growling in her stomach, Lucy took the first step towards the rehearsal wing. Her head whipped around fast when a voice called from behind her.

"Who are you?" the low timbre voice called, sending a shiver through Lucy.

She froze from the shock, but it lasted only a second before she spun around on her feet to see a tall man across the hall, walking towards her.

"Who are you? And what do you want here?" he asked again when he got to her. His lips were pulled back as his eyes narrowed on hers, and deep lines marred his smooth forehead.

Lucy hadn't seen the man before, but the frown on his face eased off when she mentioned her name. "Lucy Hale," she said, sticking a handout. "I sold treats here at the theater a few days back during the auditions."

"I remember you," he replied, but ignored her hand, so she withdrew it, and stuck it into the pocket of her coat. "Why are you here? There're no auditions and you don't have treats on you to sell, do you?"

Lucy forced on a smile even though she didn't appreciate the hint of sarcasm laced in his question. "I thought the auditions were still ongoing, so I dropped by."

He looked at her again, and Lucy also took in his features. He was several inches taller than her, so she had to angle her head a bit to get a good look at his face. His square-shaped jaw slacked a bit when his frown faded, and she noticed he had a jagged scar on the left side of his cheek.

"You want to audition?" he retorted, accessing her with his probing brown eyes. "You don't strike me like an actress, Miss Hale."

Lucy shook her head. "I'm not here to audition." She looked around where they stood. "I saw a flier showing dates for special auditions."

"It's an old one… The company in charge of distributing them might have continued without realizing Pete died."

His icy tone compelled Lucy to ask more questions. She noticed he shifted his weight from one foot to the other before speaking again.

"I'm Tim Humphrey, by the way, and I have to compliment you, Miss Hale. The treats you serve are the best. I enjoyed them, but I'm afraid coming here was a mistake… you shouldn't even have considered that the auditions would continue after what happened to Pete. If you ask me, I think it's good riddance."

Lucy lifted a brow. "Good riddance?"

"Pete was a terrible boss," Tim continued. "Many didn't like him, and I can tell you, he had it coming. If it didn't happen that day, someone else would have done it."

"Are you saying you think someone here killed him? One of the actors? Or someone else close to him?"

A muscle ticked in the side of Tim's jaw as it hardened. Lucy saw something flash in his eyes. Anger... she couldn't explain the expression he wore, but from the set line of his jaw, and the way his eyes darted away from hers then back, she could tell Tim had a lot on his mind about the murder.

Her breath hitched in her throat when she thought, *Oh Lord, could he be the killer?*

The thought swam in her head for a millisecond as she stared at Tim.

He looked into her eyes, keeping his hard look. "I have nothing to say... the cops will find out what happened, so I think you should leave."

Lucy backed away from him, walked out of the theater to her car, and drove away. His sudden change in mood made it look like he had something to hide, but she didn't want to make any assumptions.

But what if he's the killer? What motive would Tim Humphrey have to kill Pete?

From her conversation with Tim, it was obvious he disliked Pete, and Lucy even sensed that he was pleased with what happened. His words made his dislike clear. But was Tim the kind of man with the guts to kill?

She couldn't tell because she didn't know him at all. But... Tim Humphrey looked guilty to her... his shiftiness and dismissiveness made it look like he had something to hide, and if Lucy was a cop, she would investigate him.

But I'm not a cop, she reminded herself. Best to let the professionals handle the case.

She arrived at the bakery a few minutes later, and Hannah was wiping the tables when she walked in.

"Hey," Lucy said as she got out of her coat and hung it. "Sorry for taking time. I dropped by the hospital to see Aunt Tricia and stopped by the local theater. Hope it wasn't too hectic here at the bakery?"

"Not at all," Hannah replied. "It's not been frantic today, but we had a few customers drop in, and we've sold out all the waffles and brownies, so we need more for tomorrow. How is Aunt Tricia, by the way? I plan to visit her this evening on my way home."

"She's better," Lucy answered. "I planned to bake some cookies. I've been craving some. We will add brownies and waffles to the list," Lucy replied.

Hannah walked to the counter to drop the napkin she held and added as she rounded it. "Also, there's someone here to see you. She came in a few minutes ago, and it's a good thing you didn't take long to show up as she insisted on waiting for you," Hannah pointed at a woman at the extreme right end of the bakery with her back to them. Lucy looked and saw the woman sitting with her back straight and hands on the table.

"Who is it?" Lucy whispered as she walked towards the woman with Hannah by her side.

14

"It's Thelma Cousins," Hannah replied as Lucy got to the table where the woman sat. Thelma immediately rose to her feet when Lucy got to her and extended her hand.

"Hi, I'm Thelma," she said in a steady voice.

Lucy thought she oozed the charm and confidence of a Hollywood celebrity, and she remembered something about Judy saying her daughter was still an actress.

"I'm here to see the owner of the bakery," Thelma said when Lucy sat with her. "Do you have any idea when she'll be back?"

"I'm the owner," Lucy replied, crossing her fingers in front of her. "I'm Lucy Hale."

"Oh, thank goodness you're back in time. I was hoping I wouldn't wait here too long." Thelma grinned this time before she adjusted herself in her seat and ran a hand over the sleeve of her blouse. "I'm Judy Cousins' daughter, and I saw you at my mother's shop a few days ago," she began, not taking a break before she launched right into the reason she was there to see Lucy. "I was wondering if I could work for you. It will only be for two weeks, and from what I've heard about your bakery and what I can see, it will be really nice to work here."

Lucy leaned further on her chair as she accessed Thelma. Her bright countenance was probably one of her best qualities, and the charming smile she wore might get her a lot of roles, but Lucy thought it couldn't land her this job.

"I'm not in need of an extra hand now," Lucy replied, slowly getting her words out as Thelma's smile dropped. "It's still early in the year, and there's no major event going on for now. Also, I don't think you have the particular set of skills for this kind of job."

Thelma lit up again at the mention of skills. "Actually… it's more like an internship for me. I'm playing the role of small-town baker in a Denver production, and hands on experience of what it's like to work in a bakery would be helpful. I like to get into my role and play it like it's my life. I don't know if this makes sense to you."

"It does," Lucy replied, reconsidering. "So, you're looking for experience as a baker… to help with your role?"

"Exactly," Thelma replied. "It will only be for two weeks, and I don't even need to get paid. I think it'll be fun working with you, Lucy," Thelma said, then leaned closer to add. "Besides, I have connections with cool people, and celebrities, and if I put in a word about your bakery, you'll be getting lots of attention. Pretty soon, you might even look at opening multiple branches."

Lucy rolled the idea over in her head for a short time. "It sounds like a good idea," she replied. I'm not so hyped about her celebrity connections, and I'm the one who'll be doing her the favor if she works here.

Thelma clapped her hands together in excitement and chuckled as she tossed some part of her hair over her shoulder in a glamorous style.

"This will look good on my Instagram timeline," she said. "A few snapshots of the bakery and the wonderful service you offer is more than enough to drag customers here, but of course, that will only be after I'm done with the internship," she said.

Lucy smiled at her. "I will offer you a stipend for interning here," she said. "It's not right to let you work for free."

"Ahh, you're very kind."

Lucy saw her glance around the bakery again. When her gaze landed back on Lucy's, she was rising to her feet and thanking her.

When Thelma left the bakery, Hannah came to where Lucy sat and joined her. "I think this is a bad idea," she said, looking directly at Lucy. "Thelma is more of a socialite... she pulls a crowd but I sincerely doubt she'll be of any help here even as an intern... she might just be extra weight."

"Well, you were right when you said she pulls a crowd, and I think the bakery needs some media attention. Besides... she might know something about Pete's murder."

Hannah sighed, and to ease her mind a little, Lucy suggested. "Let's bake some brownies and cookies."

She led Hannah into the kitchen, and they threw themselves into work. By evening, when she closed the bakery, she was exhausted. She went to her apartment upstairs and threw herself on the couch with a loud sigh.

Gigi was immediately by her side, purring and clamoring for attention, so Lucy stroked her fur a bit.

"I'm so tired, Gigi," she muttered, closing her eyes. She was still dressed in her work outfit, and even kicking off her shoes seemed like too much work. Lucy took off the boots, and the shawl wrapped around her neck.

She turned on the television, went into her bathroom for a quick hot shower, and when she returned to the living room, the 9pm news had begun.

Lucy sat with a glass of fruit juice and crossed her legs on the center table close to the couch, where she relaxed. Gigi climbed onto the couch to stay close to her, and she brought her pet close, patting her as they listened to the news.

The report talked about Pete's murder, and a few minutes into the report, there was a sudden cut to a female reporter in front of an old building. The woman who came on the screen spoke with a slight shrill in her voice, immediately capturing Lucy's attention.

The fatigue she felt earlier was being replaced by an interest in the news report, and she massaged the back of her neck as she listened, her eyes glued to the television screen.

"We're live at the local police station in Ivy Creek, and the cops here are reluctant to release any information," the reporter was saying. "Everyone wants to know what happened to Pete Jenson, the Broadway producer, and the authorities are being highly secretive about the investigation. The lack of transparency in this investigation is worrying. We hope genuine efforts are being made to find the killer."

Lucy had never seen the reporter on the channel before, and she read the words below the clip - Stephanie Appleby, Hollywood Investigative Journalist and Reporter.

The dark-haired woman continued speaking, and Lucy paid attention.

"Ivy Creek might look serene, but looks obviously can be deceiving," she continued. "Regardless of the excellent reports we've heard about this remote Colorado town, the public now knows that the town is harboring secrets and a murderer."

A footage of the scene at the police station came up next, and as the rowdy voices of the reporters' asking questions played on the television, Lucy turned to her cat. "This is bad, Gigi," she mumbled. "Really… Pete's death is creating a ruckus. This case is dragging the town's name in the mud," she murmured.

Gigi kept looking at Lucy, her ears perked up like she understood what Lucy was saying.

"We need to do something before things get worse. Our town's good name will be tainted if the killer isn't found soon."

Gigi purred, and Lucy closed her eyes. She zoned her mind out of what the news report was saying, and as she dozed off to sleep, she replayed all she had found out so far in her mind. She planned to check on Taylor and see if she could find anything out from his end.

We need to find the killer before things become worse, and Ivy Creek becomes the most unpopular town in the country. That won't be good for anyone.

15

The next morning, Lucy and Hannah had finished baking new batches of waffles and cupcakes for the day. Lucy sat on a stool in the kitchen, her back to the door as she enjoyed the lemon tea Hannah had made. "This is amazing," she said as she sipped again. "I want to have it every day."

Hannah was bent over in front of the oven, checking the cupcakes. When she straightened, she took off the gloves she wore, dropped them on the table and placed her palm flat on it. "It's almost opening time, and your new intern isn't here. I told you this was a bad idea," she said.

"Come on, Hannah. Quit being so grumpy," Lucy said as she rose to her feet and set her mug on the table. She walked over to where Hannah was and put her hand on her shoulder. "She'll come… she'll be here."

They heard the front bell ding then, and Lucy rushed out to the dining area with Hannah to see Thelma strolling into the bakery, a wide smile on her face, and phone in one hand.

"All right, I'll talk to you later... Bye."

Thelma ended her call and slipped her phone into the pocket of the fur coat she wore. "Hi, Lucy," she said in a cheery tone, adjusting the sleeve of her coat. "How's it going?"

Thelma blinked as she spoke, still grinning, and Lucy glanced over her head to see the look on Hannah's face. She sighed, rolled her eyes, and faced Thelma again. "You're late on your first day, not a good impression."

Lucy crossed her hands over her chest and Thelma began taking off her coat. "I'm sorry, but I'm here now," she said in a sing-song voice as she walked over to the stand to hang her coat. "We can start."

"You're late, and I won't tolerate lateness, Thelma. We keep to time here."

"I'm sorry," Thelma replied, lowering her head a bit. "It won't happen again, I promise."

Hannah had gone back into the kitchen, so Lucy took Thelma around to show her the basic setting of the bakery. She showed her the price list and pointed out the packages she usually added as a side-order or a freebie when she had a customer who bought a lot from her.

"We sometimes get online orders through calls on this phone, so if you ever pick up, all you need to do is scribble down the order and get it to me or Hannah."

Thelma nodded. "Hannah's your..." She dragged out the sentence for a second.

Lucy answered, interrupting her. "Hannah's my assistant. She handles things when I'm not around, and she's here if you don't understand anything."

Thelma put on a sly smile, then leaned closer to Lucy. "I don't think she likes me very much," she whispered, a mischievous look in her eye. Lucy ignored her and turned around to walk into the kitchen and continue their tour.

The first customer for the day came in when they finished going around the kitchen. Lucy went behind the counter to attend to the man while Thelma leaned over the wall and took out her phone to text again.

She noticed Hannah staring at Thelma as she served cupcakes, and Lucy shook her head. Lucy moved closer to Hannah and poked her in the side gently. "It's only for two weeks," she said.

Hannah exhaled and went into the kitchen. The morning was busy, and by the time Lucy finally had time to rest, it was nearly mid-day. She turned on the speaker to listen to some music for a bit while she relaxed.

Thelma immediately put her phone in her pocket and came to the counter. "These are your famous waffles," she began. "I'm not so into baking, but I'd definitely like to learn how to make these."

"During interning, aren't you supposed to be actually learning?" Hannah asked in a low tone. Thelma rubbed her palms together as she stared at the waffles, and Lucy noticed Hannah's frown deepened.

"Hannah, we should check on the bread dough," she said, trying to lure Hannah into the kitchen.

Lucy walked into the kitchen first, and Hannah followed, closing the door behind her.

"All right, I sense something else is going on here, between you and Thelma," she said. "Care to share?"

Hannah dragged her fingers through her hair and rubbed her lips. "When we were in high school, Thelma and I were in the same year, and we used to be friends at some point. At least I thought we were, but turned out she was just using me to make herself more famous. She didn't really like me as a friend, and all I did was follow her around like a fool till I realized I was just her puppet."

"I'm so sorry to hear this, Hannah," Lucy said in a solemn voice. She put a hand over Hannah's shoulder and pulled her in for a hug.

"Yeah, I got over it a long time ago, but I can tell you, Thelma isn't the person you want to work with."

Lucy heard a clang from outside and rushed out of the door to check on what was happening. Thelma was standing outside, a pale look on her face as Lucy dashed past her.

"Did you break something?" she asked.

Thelma shook her head in response and pointed at the paper bag on the counter. "I was trying to pack an order for a customer."

Lucy sighed and finished packing the items for the customer. When she collected the payment from the customer and turned to find Thelma, she saw her standing by the light stand in a corner and taking a selfie.

The phone suddenly rang, distracting Lucy before she could say anything. She picked it up before it rang again.

"Yes, I have waffles and brownies available for delivery. All right, I will get down to your address and you will have them in a few minutes."

Lucy scribbled down the address, thanked the caller, and went into the kitchen to prepare it.

"Hannah, help me with the delivery basket, please," Lucy said as she counted the packed waffles to make sure it was complete. When Hannah brought the basket, she arranged them inside, and hurried out to pick some freebies.

When she got to the dining area, Thelma was standing by the door again, her hands twisting in front of the other.

"Why don't you help Hannah in the kitchen, Thelma?" Lucy said. "You shouldn't be out here staring at nothing."

"I wasn't staring, I just…" Thelma turned and pointed at a woman standing with her back to the counter. "A customer came in," she said. "She's famous."

The woman turned around at that moment, and Lucy's eyes widened when she recognized her as the reporter on the news the previous night.

"Oh my God, that's Stephanie Appleby."

"Yes," Thelma said, looking starstruck.

"She looks smaller in person, though," Lucy commented as she looked at the woman again.

"Well, there's a saying that TV puts weight on you or something along those lines," Thelma replied.

"I'll go talk to her." Lucy went to the woman and tapped her lightly on the shoulder. "Hi, would you like something to eat?"

"Yes, please, but as soon as I finish this call," Stephanie replied with a pleasant smile before returning her attention to her phone.

Lucy left her and returned to the kitchen to pick up the basket she had put together. Hannah was washing her hands at the sink when she entered.

"Guess who we have as a customer today," Lucy announced when she got to her. "Celebrity reporter Stephanie Appleby."

Lucy wondered what had brought a Hollywood celebrity to her bakery.

Did she get referred here by someone? Is she here on official business or to buy some of my treats?

"You're kidding," Hannah replied, turning to her.

"You should go see for yourself then."

"Holy…" Hannah exclaimed. "What do we do? We should do something, right? Is everything set? We have enough pastries for sale?"

Hannah was rambling, and Lucy put her hands on Hannah's shoulders to calm her.

Lucy said, "Relax… Everything is set, and we're always ready to welcome any customer."

Hannah sucked in a deep breath and nodded. "All right," she murmured.

"I will go deliver these, so you will be here to take her order when she's ready to make one. I don't think we should leave Thelma out there with the customers alone because—"

A crashing thud from the dining area interrupted Lucy's sentence. She moved spontaneously, dashing out of the kitchen with Hannah behind her to see what was happening.

16

What in heaven's name happened? Lucy wondered as she dashed into the dining area with Hannah behind her. "What was that?" she asked, her heart in her throat as she rounded the corner and stopped in her tracks when she saw Stephanie standing with both hands over her mouth.

Thelma stood frozen to a spot in front of the broken vase, a horrified look on her face, and Lucy repeated her question to get her attention.

"Oh my God," Stephanie exclaimed before Thelma could reply. Stephanie dropped her hands and angled her body to face Thelma.

Stephanie's brows knotted into a frown, and she jabbed a finger at Thelma as she continued. "You almost killed me."

Lucy looked from Thelma to Stephanie, trying to understand what had happened with the broken vase on the floor.

"I'm so sorry," Thelma blurted just before Stephanie huffed, adjusted her shoulder bag, and hurried out of the bakery. When the door closed behind her, Lucy folded her arms over her chest, arched a brow and faced Thelma.

Thelma shuddered and squeezed her eyes shut for a second. "I didn't try to kill her, I swear it," she said when she re-opened them.

Hannah stood at the kitchen's entrance, her hand folded over her chest, and Lucy saw her shrug and walk back into the kitchen before she faced Thelma again.

"What happened?" she asked, contemplating dashing out of the bakery after Stephanie. "How did you break the vase?"

"I'm sorry… I noticed it was out of place, and I was trying to fix it, but it just dropped, and I couldn't stop the fall. Please, trust me."

Lucy sighed. She pushed her fingers through her hair and rubbed her forehead for a second. "Stephanie's a famous reporter from the city, and whatever she tells the world about Sweet Delights is definitely going to stick. Your clumsiness might ruin my business," she scolded.

Thelma lowered her head, and Lucy released another sigh before she walked past Thelma and headed out of the bakery to find Stephanie. She didn't think Stephanie would have gone far, so she doubled her steps, hoping to find her.

As a one-time food critic, Lucy was mindful of her customer service because she knew what a critical review could do for a business. Especially one from someone as influential as Stephanie Appleby.

Lucy walked down the first three blocks she passed, scanning her surroundings to see if Stephanie had entered one of the local shops around. She passed a diner and noticed a crowd of locals in front of a bookstore across the street from her.

When she crossed over to the other side, Lucy noticed they were staring at Stephanie inside the bookstore through the windows. Stephanie seemed engrossed in a conversation with a lady, probably the store's manager. She was holding a book in one hand, making hand gestures with the other as she spoke, and it reminded Lucy of the news report she watched the previous night.

Lucy lifted a hand to rub the back of her neck as she made her way into the store. It's best I apologize to her. I don't need the bakery getting the wrong review from a reporter.

Inside the store, she approached Stephane immediately as the lady walked away from her.

"Hi," Lucy said when she drew closer. She slipped her hands into the pocket of the jeans she wore and continued. "I'm so sorry about what happened at my bakery earlier. Thelma, the lady you met, is an actress, interning there to learn some skills for her next role as a baker, so she really does not know about baking or customer service."

Lucy noticed Stephanie took a step back at first before speaking. "Really?" she asked.

"Yes, really… it was an accident, so I came here to apologize."

"Alright then, water under the bridge."

Relief flooded Lucy, and she released an audible sigh. "Great. I'm Lucy, by the way… Lucy Hale. I'm Sweet Delights owner."

"Nice to meet you, Lucy," Stephanie responded. "I'm Steph."

Lucy gave a soft nod before her gaze dropped to the book Stephanie held in her right hand. She read the title quickly and looked Stephanie in the eye. "That's an enjoyable book you're holding there."

"It is?"

Lucy responded with a nod. "I've read the first two parts. It's a trilogy, and it has one of the best plots if you ask me. You won't regret getting or reading it."

"Thank goodness. I was having second thoughts about getting it because it's an author I don't know but getting a review from someone who's read it has definitely cemented my decision."

Lucy noticed it was quite easy to get into a conversation with her.

"I read it in an entire day when I first got it, didn't want to put it down for a second. If you get it, I'm sure you'll feel the same way about the story."

"It's a good way to pass time," Stephanie said, continuing their conversation. "Especially in an uneventful town like this. I mean, how slow can time pass? I've been out and about since dawn broke and it's not even twelve noon yet," she said with a laugh as she glanced at her watch.

"Ivy Creek isn't so bad… this is actually a peaceful place to be in," Lucy replied.

"You sound like you've lived here a long time," Stephanie said as she picked up two more books and accessed them.

"I was born here. Ivy Creek is my home."

"So, you probably know or have met Pete Jenson?"

The question reminded Lucy that the lady was a reporter when she threw the bold question. "Yes, I met Pete Jenson a few times before the incident," she admitted.

"What did you think of him? And the incident?" Stephanie probed.

"Well, I didn't know him so well, but I know a few things. Most people here believed he always put the town down when he had time to speak about us, and that made him disliked by many. Also, I got to find out that he never appreciated talent from town, and always tried to cheat the people he worked with. Either way, I think what happened is a genuine tragedy. No one deserves to die like that."

"Right," Stephanie said. "It was nice speaking to you, Lucy," she added. "I'll drop by your bakery before I leave Ivy Creek. Hopefully, that won't be long from now."

"Thank you," Lucy replied as she shook hands with her. "It's a pleasure talking to you."

"Same."

She watched Stephanie walk to the counter to pay for her books and faced the shelf to scout for a contemporary novel that could keep her busy during her leisure time on Sundays. After a quick search, Lucy settled for a crime thriller. She paid for the book in cash, then headed out of the store and back to the bakery.

When she entered, she noticed Hannah was alone at the counter, attending to customers, and Thelma was nowhere in sight.

"How did it go with Stephanie?" Hannah asked as Lucy joined her after putting the novel she bought in her office.

"Turns out she's really nice. I apologized, we chatted a little, and she even said she would drop by sometime."

"Thank goodness it went well," Hannah replied as she accepted cash from a customer. "Would have been a real disaster if you didn't get to her in time, and if the bakery got a bad review from a famous reporter, that would have been Thelma's fault."

Lucy understood why Hannah was always harsh with Thelma, and she also thought Thelma needed to take her internship seriously.

"I don't think she can commit to this position, and she might actually ruin things for me," Lucy admitted to Hannah. "I guess maybe you were right about her."

Hannah went into the kitchen to check on the muffins in the oven while Lucy continued attending to the customers in line.

The rest of the day, Lucy attended to the customers in line and made one delivery to the town's hospital before she closed the bakery for the day.

On the news that night, the town's deputy sheriff, Taylor, was on the news with a local reporter.

"The investigation is still ongoing, and the department asks for all citizens of Ivy Creek to remain calm and patient. We will find the perpetrators of this heinous crime and justice will be served."

Lucy hoped there would be a quick resolution to the murder investigation as the good name of Ivy Creek was hanging in the balance.

17

The next morning, Lucy hummed a song to herself as she strolled around the counters in the grocery store. She had picked a basketful of cooking ingredients for her kitchen, and now she needed to get some baking soda for the bakery.

When she finished picking the items on her list, she rolled her cart towards the front.

She had woken up that morning with the urge to do something brand new, and a lemon meringue pie seemed like a good way to start the day.

I will put some on sale to see how much the customers like it, she thought as she rolled her cart forward when it got to her turn.

"Hi," Lucy greeted the cashier.

The woman grinned as she looked up from her computer screen, but her grin slowly faded when she looked at Lucy, and her lips formed a tight line. Lucy wondered if she caused the cashier's change in demeanor.

Behind Lucy, two women argued between themselves. Lucy heard her name and glanced over her shoulder to look at them.

"It's her, Lucy Hale, the owner of the bakery," one of them murmured, eyeing Lucy with a nasty look.

"That will be fifty dollars, please," the cashier said, dragging Lucy's attention back to her.

Lucy tapped her fingers on the counter before she reached into the pocket of her coat for her wallet. She noticed to her side an elderly man glare at her. His eyes fixed on hers for a second when she looked at him, and he only turned away when a younger boy steered him away from where he stood.

Is something wrong with my dress? Lucy wondered, feeling self-conscious. She gave the cashier a shaky smile, took out cash to pay for her items, and waited for her change.

"Thank you," Lucy said when the cashier handed her the shopping bags.

"I thought you loved Ivy Creek," the cashier said, shaking her head.

Lucy looked behind her to see if the cashier was talking to someone else.

"Hello, let me check that for you," the cashier continued, turning her attention to the next person on the line, and forcing Lucy to step away.

Gathering her bags, she walked away from the counter, still analyzing what the cashier meant by her statement. When Lucy walked out of the store, she went to the first car she saw parked. She checked her face in the side mirror to see if anything was amiss.

"Why is everyone staring at me?" she wondered out loud. Straightening again, she scanned the surrounding area where she stood, noticing that some people who walked into the store stopped to stare at her and murmur to themselves.

Rubbing her forehead, Lucy started her walk back to the bakery. It was only a short distance away, and she had planned to get back in time to work on the lemon pie before noon.

When she crossed the road and took the street leading to her bakery, she glanced at her watch to make sure she was still on time. A few minutes' walk down the street, and Lucy saw Richard jogging down the road.

She stopped walking when he drew closer to her, slowing down his pace but not stopping entirely.

"Hey," Lucy said. She hadn't seen him in days since her last visit to his cafeteria, and Richard hadn't bothered to call either. "I haven't seen or heard from you in a while… How are you?"

"Great… you seem good too," he replied, jogging on a spot as he talked.

Lucy watched him wipe a hand over the sweat on his forehead.

"The entire town's talking about you. At least now you're certain your bakery is going to get a lot of media attention."

Lucy arched a brow in confusion. "What are you talking about?"

"I can't slow down. Maybe we'll talk later?" Richard responded and resumed his jog. He waved at her briefly, and her gaze followed him as he continued down the street.

Lucy was still frowning when she continued her walk back to the bakery.

What a weird day, she thought. Inside the bakery, Lucy set the bags down in the kitchen and took out her mixer to prepare her pie when her phone pinged in the back pocket of her jeans.

She got two texts from Hannah and Aunt Tricia. She opened the latter first.

> **Thanks for the flowers and for showing up the other day. Will you come around this evening? It'll be fun to have someone around for the last round of tests before I get discharged.**

Shaking her head, Lucy quickly replied to her aunt.

> **Yes, sure! I'll try to round up at the bakery in time to be there with you.**

She read Hannah's text next.

> **Hey Lucy, could you please text me the recipe for the coffee cake? I want to make some at home today.**

The text reminded Lucy that it was Hannah's free day. She sighed as she looked around the kitchen, remembering that she would have to handle things on her own all day. The chances of Thelma also coming in for work were slim. Since she took off yesterday, Lucy hadn't seen or heard from her.

Lucy texted Hannah the recipe, then began preparing her lemon pie.

She was glad when her first customer of the day walked through her doors.

"Good morning," Lucy said with enthusiasm as she placed both hands flat on the counter. "What would you like?"

The woman looked around the bakery, and when her gaze landed on Lucy's again, Lucy sensed there was a bit of hesitation in the way she looked at the display glass of pastries.

"Seems like you're having a slow day," the woman commented as she looked at Lucy again, shaking her head.

Lucy kept her smile, trying not to appear too worried about the lack of activity in her bakery. It was nearly past eleven am, and she just got her first customer for the day.

Something seems off today. It all started at the grocery store she had visited earlier that day. With everyone staring at her, the cashier's weird comment, and the run-in with Richard on the street, Lucy could only conclude that she was having a very peculiar day. She just hoped things would return to normal... fast.

"Perhaps people need a brief break from treats, but they'll be back," she replied with optimism. "In the meantime, what can I get you? You should try our lemon meringue pie... I'm sure you'll like it."

"Sure, let me have that," the woman replied, tapping her fingers against the counter as Lucy began packing her order. She paid in cash and walked out of the store.

Lucy dropped to a stool behind her and exhaled deeply. What's happening today? She was still wondering why she had no customers when the door opened again.

This time, it was Taylor who walked in, and Lucy was on her feet before he got to the counter.

"Hey," he said. "Busy day?"

"Not in the least. Would you believe I haven't had more than a customer all day? It's really a slow day. People have been funny to me all day, too."

"Funny?" Taylor asked.

She looked at him, noticing his interest in what she was saying, as he fixed his eyes on her face.

"Yes," she answered. "I had people stare at me all day in the grocery store, and on the street. It made me feel green… like an alien who just landed from outer space." Lucy shuddered as she spoke and wrapped her arms around her chest.

"Maybe you caused it," Taylor said with a shrug. Lines pulled at the corner of his mouth. "I mean, why else would everyone be so interested in staring at you if you haven't done or said something? You know how people love to gossip around here… but there's no smoke without fire."

Lucy chuckled at his turn of phrase, and he laughed with her for a second before clearing his throat.

"I'm serious, Lucy," he added. His voice remained soft as he spoke.

What could I have done?

"What do you mean? I don't think there's anything interesting I've done recently."

Taylor shook his head. He reached into his pocket and took out his phone. "It's best if I show you," he explained in a low voice, his eyes soft on hers.

Lucy's heart pounded in her chest as she waited, watching him scroll through his phone for whatever he was about to show her.

18

Taylor moved closer to the counter for Lucy to get a closer look. Her eyes widened as she read the headlines linked to the video.

"This is trending?" she asked Taylor, dismayed at the news she was watching.

"The owner of the local second-rate bakery, Sweet Delights, told me personally that many people in this town didn't have many good things to say about the deceased. It makes me wonder if this murder was planned and supported by some locals," Stephanie was saying in a news report. "This local baker, Lucy Hale, boldly mentioned that Pete Jenson wasn't exactly loved by the members of this town."

Stephanie quoted Lucy's statement about Pete belittling the town and watching this made Lucy's jaw drop.

"Everyone has probably seen this clip," Lucy muttered as Stephanie's words faded in her ears.

"Yes, this broke out on the local news channel late last night, and it's been trending around town since morning. I'm surprised you didn't know or see this on the news."

"I haven't watched the news all day," Lucy replied and fixed her attention on the video again.

She listened to Stephanie spout more untruths about Ivy Creek.

"I don't think Ivy Creek is peaceful at all. If anything, I think they are a bunch of hypocrites."

Lucy turned away from Taylor and shoved her hands through her hair, sighing in frustration. Taylor paused the video when she faced him again, shaking her head.

"I would never say a thing like that about this town. That woman is completely taking what I told her out of context."

Taylor was quiet, and Lucy replayed what had happened at the grocery store earlier that morning. It made sense now why she was getting all those icy stares and whispers from people around, and Richard's comment about her business strategy.

"This will ruin my reputation and business in town," she continued as she started to pace. "I can't believe this. I've gotten myself involved in another investigation again. This time around, the backlash might be hostile."

"Hey… hey," Taylor said.

She turned to him as he slipped his phone into his pocket and met her gaze. His eyes were soft on hers as he spoke.

"Nothing like that is going to happen. This is just a rumor, and the view of one investigative journalist who is not even a member of our community. I know you would never speak ill of our town, and I'm sure there are others who know this, too."

His words had a relaxing effect on her, and Lucy's shoulders dropped as the worse of her worries faded. Still, she had to find a way to make sure Stephanie corrected her public statement about her.

"I won't sit back and let her ruin my reputation. There must be a way to make sure she says the truth and tell everyone that I never said any of those things or insinuated that Pete was murdered by someone here in Ivy Creek. Besides, I would never give a customer any bad experience here at Sweet Delights."

It was Taylor's turn to sigh. "You shouldn't worry so much, Lu… this will blow over soon," Taylor consoled.

He smiled at her, the corners of his eyes crinkling up as he did. "The storm will be over soon, and you'll be able to get back to business as usual. So far, you've done great, and this little issue won't change all the hard work. Trust me."

Lucy returned his smile, her heart warming up at his confidence. Hearing encouraging words from him relieved some of the tension already growing on her shoulders.

To her surprise, Taylor reached over the counter and put a hand over hers on the counter. The contact lasted briefly, and her skin tingled as he pulled away.

"Once the investigation ends, everyone will return to their lives and all of this will be history."

"Thanks for your kind words, Taylor," she said after a second of silence passed between them again. "It means a lot."

"It's nothing…" he answered. "I know how hard you've worked since you returned, and I admire your dedication. You should keep the hard work going, and soon this place will be bigger than you imagined."

"Would you like some lemon pie?" Lucy asked. "I made some this morning. I think you should try it and take some home to your mom."

Lucy was already packing him three slices of pie as she spoke, and he thanked her when she handed it over to him.

"I'll see you around," she called after him as he waved at her, then made his way out of the bakery.

Alone again, Lucy sat on the stool behind her and closed her eyes for a second. What a disaster, she thought, mortified at how things had turned out with Stephanie. After their conversation, and with Stephanie promising to drop by the bakery sometime later, Lucy had thought things were off to a smooth start with the reporter.

She can ruin everything I've worked so hard to build here with her words.

Lucy was lost in her thoughts for the next hour, and the alarm she set on her phone to remind her of her visit to the hospital dragged her out of it.

No one had walked into the store or called to place any order all day, and frankly, she was exhausted from the waiting.

Lucy got on her feet, cleaned the counter, and packed up for the day. She closed the bakery after a quick drop into her apartment upstairs to feed Gigi, and drove out, heading for the hospital.

Lucy drove onto the main street, her attention on the road and the incidents of the past twenty-four hours.

How much will this affect me? She thought as she turned into Easton Street and stepped on the brakes when the traffic light turned red.

To clear her head, she turned on the radio, hoping to listen to some music, but Stephanie's clear tone hit her ears the minute she tuned in.

"The owner of the local second-rate bakery, Lucy Hale, specifically told me that the town members didn't exactly like or worship Pete Jenson…"

Lucy rolled her eyes. Is she saying this on every channel?

She changed the station to one playing music and spent the rest of the drive singing along to the pop songs. Lucy dropped by Judy's store to get her aunt flowers and for her apartment.

Something colorful and fresh will brighten my mood. Aunt Tricia had loved the last flowers she had gotten, so she would get the same ones for her.

Lucy parked by the side of the road across from Judy's store and got out.

She slipped her hands into the pocket of her coat as she crossed and strode towards the entrance. Through the windows, she spotted Judy bent over a pot of flowers, inhaling their scent.

Judy straightened and turned in her direction as she stepped over the threshold, and Lucy quickly put on a smile.

"Hey, Judy," she said in a light tone, tucking the loose strands of hair falling to the side of her face behind her right ear. "How're you doing?"

"You again?" Judy said in a stern voice.

Lucy froze at the unwelcome response. Judy's frown deepened, marring her facial features, and Lucy's heart pounded in her chest as Judy folded her arms over her chest and spat in a gruff tone. "What do you want?"

Woah! Seems like I've become public enemy number one, Lucy thought, blinking and reeling in shock at the hostile welcome from Judy Cousins.

19

"What do you want?" Judy asked again, her blazing eyes fixed on Lucy for a second. Lucy paused in her stride as she reeled from the unexpected cold welcome from Judy.

Without a word, she spun around to walk out of the store, but gasped when she saw Tim Humphrey standing behind her, a grim expression on his face.

"I was talking to Tim," Judy said again, making Lucy turn back to face her.

"You can stay Lucy, I was asking Tim to leave, not you."

Tim Humphrey took another step forward into the store, despite Judy's instruction. He clenched his hands at his side, and Lucy didn't miss the obvious tension in the air between them.

"You're kicking me out now?" Tim retorted. "You promised to settle everything the next time I came here, and now you're pretending you don't know what I want?"

Judy's eyes widened and darted across the room to Lucy's. "I don't know what you're talking about," she denied, dropping the flower she held carelessly on the table.

Lucy remained on the same spot, watching Judy close the distance between her and Tim. Judy raised her chin defiantly as she spoke to him. "I want you to leave my store right now. Let's not cause a scene, please."

A long minute of silence festered in the store, then Tim raised both hands in a gesture of surrender.

"Right," he spat as he backed away. "Don't come running to me for help when next you need it."

Tim cast one sideways glance at Lucy before he walked out of the store. Judy faced her then, released a shuddering breath and pushed back the strands of hair falling to the side of her face.

"Sorry, you shouldn't have seen that," she said, angling her body towards Lucy. "He's come here three times in the last week, and I don't know what he wants. I don't want to have anything to do with Tim Humphrey, especially now that the cops are investigating him for Pete's murder."

The cops are investigating Tim. Lucy pondered on this fresh development as she listened to Judy complain.

"Sorry if it came off like I was kicking you out of my store. I wouldn't do that…"

Lucy adjusted her bag on her shoulder. She followed Judy to the counter when she walked away.

"Maybe he needs something from you," Lucy said. "Have you tried figuring out what that is?"

Judy shook her head in response. "He did some gardening for me a few weeks ago, and I paid him for it, but he's demanding more money. I'm all for helping people, but my generosity will not be used to blackmail me."

Lucy nodded, noting Judy's judgement of Tim. She could understand where Judy was coming from regarding not letting one's kindness be abused by other people. For a second, she contemplated asking Judy about what Tim meant, but changed her mind when she remembered her decision not to involve herself in this investigation.

Judy was already gathering the flowers she dropped earlier into a vase. When she faced Lucy again, she was dusting her palms together.

"I came in for some lavender flowers," Lucy said. "My aunt loved the previous ones I got."

"I knew she would." Judy brought another bouquet and handed it to Lucy. "This should do the trick once more."

"Thanks, Judy." She collected the flowers and inhaled its scent before looking at Judy again.

"I heard about what happened with the reporter. I'm so sorry, Lucy. Thelma isn't always that clumsy. I wonder what got into her that day," Judy said.

Judy looked genuinely concerned as she spoke, worry lines forming on her forehead, and Lucy sighed.

"It's alright," Lucy replied. "What happened was an accident. It wasn't Thelma's fault entirely."

"I'm glad you think so," Judy said almost immediately as her hand flew to her cheeks. "I was so worried this would affect your working relationships," she continued. "I didn't want that to happen. It's good to know I have nothing to worry about."

Lucy cleared her throat, feeling uncomfortable with the way Judy was staring at her. She shifted her weight from one foot to the other and reached into her pocket for her wallet. "I'll take a bouquet of lilies for myself," she said as she took out some cash.

"Thanks for dropping by, Lucy," Judy said after she paid for the flowers.

"You're welcome."

Lucy was about to leave the store when the door opened, and Thelma stepped in. Thelma gasped when Lucy saw her. The bags she held dropped to the ground, and at the spur of the moment, she spun back around on her heels and ran out of the store.

"Thelma," Judy called after, but she didn't look back. Lucy saw Judy's apologetic smile when she glanced over her shoulder one last time at her. She acknowledged the smile with a nod and walked out of the store.

While heading to her car, Lucy looked around to see if she would spot Thelma. She drove off when she didn't and arrived at the hospital a few minutes later to see Aunt Tricia sitting on her bed, both hands clasped to the side of the mattress before she rose to her feet and tried to find her balance.

Lucy rushed forward to support her after dropping her bags.

"You made it," Aunt Tricia said softly.

"Yeah."

The doctor checked Aunt Tricia's ankle one last time after asking her to walk around, then he scribbled a prescription on a piece of paper and handed it to Lucy. "For her arthritis," he said. "She can go home in the morning."

"Thank you."

Lucy frowned at her aunt when they were alone. "I didn't know you had arthritis," she said, waving the paper at Aunt Tricia.

"It's not important," Aunt Tricia dismissed with a sort of laugh. "I'm just happy I finally get to go home."

Lucy sat on the bed with her and handed over the flowers she bought. "You're moving in with me, so I will keep a closer eye on you now," she said, satisfied with her decision to look after Aunt Tricia.

"How are things at the bakery?" Aunt Tricia asked. "What have I missed?"

Lucy spent the next hour telling her aunt all about the experience with Thelma and Stephanie, and what she noticed at Judy's store earlier.

It was evening when she returned to the bakery. Lucy parked her car behind the bakery and by the time she got to the front again, she saw Stephanie waiting at the door.

Stephanie seemed engrossed in her phone until Lucy drew closer to her. Her head snapped up when Lucy climbed onto the patio and stopped in front of her.

"I didn't think you'd be stopping by here," Lucy commented, allowing her eyes to drift over the woman's face. She wished she could wipe the smug smile off Stephanie's face, but that was not an option.

"Why wouldn't I be back? The locals say this place sells the best pastries in town."

Stephanie looked around and put one hand on her waist, striking a pose. "It doesn't look like there's much going on around here, anyway."

Lucy's hands formed fists at her side, and she replied through gritted teeth. "You lied in your report about what I told you. I don't remember insinuating that someone here murdered Pete."

Stephanie shrugged. "It changes nothing. We both know someone here did anyway, so what's the difference?"

"I would never speak ill about this town. You need to make this right and tell the truth."

Lucy held Stephanie's gaze for a moment. It didn't seem like Stephanie would back down. Her eyes danced with mischief as Lucy stared, and she scoffed, angled her head to one side and parted her lips in a sigh.

"I decide what I report," Stephanie began, spiking Lucy's irritation. She took a step towards Stephanie, and the blare of cop sirens behind them interrupted Lucy's attempt to tell the reporter her mind.

"Miss Appleby?" A cop called from behind them.

Lucy stepped away and turned to see three cops come out of the police car.

"What's happening?" Stephanie asked.

"We would like a word with you, please," the cop said again.

"I'll think about changing my statement," Stephanie said as she breezed past Lucy and sashayed towards the cop's vehicle.

Lucy gave her one last look as she fiddled in her bag for her keys.

She opened her bakery, got in, but moved to the window to watch Stephanie and the cops from there. Stephanie spoke to them for a while, making many hand gestures as she did before she got into the car and drove off with them.

Is she part of the investigation? Lucy wondered as she saw the car disappear into the distance.

20

Two days later, Lucy handed Aunt Tricia a cup of coffee when she joined her in the kitchen. They spent the night in her apartment upstairs, but she planned to speed things up and move back into her house before the end of the week.

"This tastes amazing," Aunt Tricia commented as she took a sip. "Soy milk?"

"Yes. A new recipe I tried out for myself. It tastes heavenly, and I think I'll be having this every morning now." She chuckled as she emptied her mug and set it on the table before moving in to have a slice of toast on the table.

"It will not be a busy day today, so I'm reaching out to Hannah's uncle, Keith, with my choice for the interior designs."

"What did you settle on?"

Lucy took out her phone, opened the brochure she spent the past few days deliberating on, and showed Aunt Tricia her top choice. "This," she said, handing the phone over to her. "This one is lovely; I think it will blend well with the colors on the wall."

"I think so too," Aunt Tricia replied.

"I already set up an appointment with Keith to come around this morning. I should call to find out if he's on his way."

Aunt Tricia went through the brochure briefly, then handed her back the phone so she could call Keith. The call lasted for a few minutes and when it was over; she emailed the cleaning agency she had contacted the previous night.

Lucy started the baking for the day when she finished the call, and Hannah joined her as soon as she arrived. They talked about the decrease in activities at the bakery for the next few weeks during the renovation, and Hannah's idea was to set up a pop-up shop in front of the bakery's building so they could serve the citizens of Ivy Creek.

Keith and his team arrived before any other customer, and Lucy quickly showed them around the bakery. The expansion would create room for a bigger kitchen, and once the apartment upstairs was gone, they could create a sales station up there for other treats she was thinking of adding to their menu for spring.

She turned to Keith when they came into the kitchen again.

"That's all I need for now. I will get back to you with a quotation and list of items needed," he said.

"Sounds like a plan," Lucy agreed with a smile.

She escorted Keith outside, handed him a free pack of cupcakes Hannah had prepared, and bade him farewell before heading back inside to meet Hannah and Aunt Tricia.

"This is finally happening," Hannah said with an excited squeal, and Lucy matched her excitement with a laugh. She heard the doorbell ding and hurried out to receive the customer.

"Hey," she greeted when she saw Taylor walk in.

He wore a casual t-shirt and shorts with a base-ball cap, and he took the cap off as he got to the counter.

"Free day?" Lucy asked.

"Yes," he replied. "I came to get some of those lovely lemon pies you made the other day, and also check on how you're doing." He looked around the dining area before his gaze settled on hers again. "How are you holding up?"

"Things are slow but great," she replied, tapping her fingers on the counter. "I'm moving forward with the expansion, and I've had someone come in to view the place and take measurements. I want it done before spring, and I'm so excited."

"I can tell you're excited," he replied. "You're doing that thing you do with your fingers when you can't keep the joy down and need to share it with someone else."

Lucy grinned. "You know me too well."

She nodded. "Let me get your order."

She packed the lemon pie and an extra cupcake for him, handed it over, and thanked him for the order. "Bye… Have a nice day."

Taylor waved at her before leaving the bakery and she returned inside to join in Hannah and Aunt Tricia's discussion about the report Stephanie made about Lucy's comment.

"It's outrageous that she could take what I said and twist it into something else," Lucy complained as they moved their discussion onto the patio. The day rolled by quickly, with only two customers besides Taylor coming in for the day.

Later that evening, Richard dropped by at the bakery. Lucy greeted him outside while Aunt Tricia and Hannah excused themselves and went inside.

"It's been a while," she said as she relaxed in her chair. "I haven't seen or heard from you since our run in on the street that morning."

Richard nodded. He sighed as he lowered himself to the chair Hannah had occupied moments earlier. "I'm sorry. I should have called or responded to your texts, but I got caught up in work."

Lucy assessed him as he apologized, and shrugged, determined to let their lack of communication slide. She hadn't thought about Richard much in the past days either. Her mind had been too pre-occupied with everything happening around her, and then there was the conversation they had at his café the last time she was there.

"I see you're moving on with the expansion as planned." He paused for a second and looked around before continuing. "You're doing just fine as you are now, and I don't understand why you need to make this bigger than it already is and risk losing what you already have."

"You're being insensitive, Richard," she pointed out in a flat voice. "The news Stephanie reported chased customers away."

I don't know if I'm more annoyed or disappointed; she thought as she looked at him.

"You know, I thought at least you would be one of the few who would believe that I'd say nothing bad about this town. You know how much this bakery means to me, and how much work I've put into it. How can you belittle my efforts?"

"Belittle? I merely stated that it was a good move, which it was. I mean Lucy, look around you. No one here cares about how big your bakery is but you."

"How can you say that? You're trying to say that I shouldn't grow?"

"It's too much pressure on you. A kind of pressure you don't need. And what if something goes wrong? You'll suffer losses. Is that what you want?'

"Oh, I get it now. It's not that you don't want me to expand… It's that you don't believe I can do it," she said and rose from her chair.

"Lucy—"

"You've said enough," she interrupted, raising a hand to stop him from proceeding. "You know what saddens me, it's that you don't think I can pull this off. I get that you're not a big fan of the expansion and everything else, but at least you could try to pretend you're happy for me and support me regardless of anything else. It's what I would have done for you."

Without another word to him, she walked away and re-entered the bakery. Aunt Tricia and Hannah probably overheard their conversation because she noticed the look of concern on their faces as she entered and hurried past them to get to her apartment upstairs.

Lucy lay in bed, focusing her mind on the business at hand and trying to ignore the obvious ache in her heart. She realized the relationship with Richard was on its last legs.

I can't be with a man who doesn't support me.

When Lucy went down to the bakery later, Hannah had closed for the day, and Aunt Tricia was sitting on the front porch enjoying a glass of cool lemonade.

"You're alright?" Aunt Tricia asked when she joined her and took a sip from the glass on the table.

"Yeah, I'll be fine," she replied. It wasn't the first time Lucy had to end a relationship with someone she really cared about, so she was certain she would recover from this one, too.

"Good, because you have a lot going on for you, Lucy, and you can't afford to get distracted. You're doing great and that matters more than anything else."

"Thanks aunt," she replied gently. "You're my rock every time I need one. I love you."

"Love you too, Lucy. Now cheer up… a smile suits you better every time," she said.

Lucy laughed then and picked up the glass again. "It sure does."

They recalled memories of Lucy's childhood in town, and the times Aunt Tricia came to visit.

It was nearly past nine pm when they retired for the night, and Lucy made sure Aunt Tricia was comfortable on the bed first before she took her spot on the couch in the living room.

She woke up to a text from Hannah the next morning, and yawned as she sat on the couch, took the phone, and read through it with sleepy eyes.

Hey, Lucy... I can't make it to the bakery this morning because I had to go to the hospital a few minutes ago. I'll talk to you when you see this.

Lucy immediately sat up on her bed, alarm bells ringing in her head as she re-read the text.

What could have happened to Hannah?

21

Lucy hurried past the nurse's station thirty minutes later. She followed the direction a nurse gave and entered the emergency ward unit. She didn't make it far before she spotted Hannah standing by a bedside.

"Hannah," she called, putting her hands on Hannah's shoulders to examine her. "You're alright? What happened?"

"I'm good," Hannah replied with a sigh. "It's Thelma who's hurt," she added.

Lucy's eyes fell on the bed then, and a pale Thelma gave her a weak smile.

"Hi Lucy," Thelma greeted. "It's me who got hurt, and Hannah was on the scene, so she volunteered to come to the hospital with me."

Lucy dropped her bag on a chair and moved to the side of the bed so she could stand beside Thelma. "Oh honey, what happened? Did you get badly hurt?'

Thelma shook her head. Lucy put a hand on the bandage on her forehead and stroked it gently. She looked at Hannah, waiting for someone to tell her how Thelma had gotten injured.

"A drunk driver hit her car from behind," Hannah said. "She hit her head on the steering wheel, and probably sustained a concussion, but besides that, the doctors say she's fine."

"Thank goodness," Lucy exclaimed. She pulled a chair close to the bed and sat. She rubbed Thelma's hand as she listened to Thelma explain what happened on the road.

"The cops arrested the culprit on the scene," Hannah added.

"I'm relieved you're all right, Thelma," Lucy said again as she looked at Thelma. "When I got the text, I thought something bad had happened."

Lucy saw Hannah glance at her watch, then at her. "Is Aunt Tricia alone at the bakery? She will need help because Uncle Keith and his team are starting work today."

"Yes, we should get back to the bakery in time before their arrival," Lucy agreed.

She gave Thelma a soft smile as she rose to her feet. "I'll come check on you in the evening."

"Lucy," Thelma called when Lucy turned to walk away with Hannah. Lucy turned back to face her. "I'm sorry about the incident with Stephanie," she apologized, hanging her head low. "I feel like it's my fault she made that report about your bakery. I should have been more careful and should have taken responsibility instead of walking away and not showing up for work."

Lucy remained quiet as Thelma apologized. Thelma's actions played a role in damaging her bakery's reputation in Ivy Creek, and she was still working on getting things back to normal. It would take a while for things to return to normal for her, yes, and she could hold that against Thelma. But that was never Lucy's approach to life.

She preferred to hope for the best and believe the best in people.

"I hope you can forgive me," Thelma repeated, this time meeting Lucy's gaze.

With a sigh, Lucy crossed over to the bed and touched Thelma's hand again, squeezing gently to show her affection. "I understand, and I forgive you. Don't worry about anything for now and focus on getting better."

"Thank you so much," Thelma said.

Lucy laughed. "Sure... I have to get back to the bakery now, but I'll come check on you later, okay?"

"Alright."

On her way out of the hospital, she spotted Taylor with some other cops questioning a doctor and waved at him briefly before exiting the building.

"I see you're getting friendlier with Taylor," Hannah commented as they drove back towards the bakery. "He drops by often and even smiles whenever he sees you."

Lucy caught Hannah's mischievous look when she stole a glance at her. She understood what it implied, and shook her head, laughing it off with a wave of her hand. "There's nothing to it. We're just getting back on good terms. When I first moved back to town, it seemed like he resented me a bit for our breakup, but I think we're past that now, and we might even be friendly neighbors now."

"That sounds good," Hannah replied with a chuckle.

Few minutes after they arrived at the bakery, she saw Keith's quote in an email.

She texted him to say that she'd get back to him shortly and then headed into the kitchen to start work for the day.

Once the expansion work started, she would have to minimize the amount of baking she did in a day because she would bake from her house, but she planned to keep the concession store and the pop-up stand running. That way, she could still make sales while expanding.

Later that evening, after the long, busy hours, she drove Aunt Tricia to her house on Easton Street and helped her settle in. She then drove to the grocery store to get some items. As she strolled around picking what she needed, she spotted Richard on the other end of a row where she stood. He looked at her for a moment before walking in her direction.

Lucy cleared her throat and kept her head high when he got to her.

"Hey," he said. His face lacked any obvious expression, so she couldn't tell what he was thinking as she looked at him. "How are you?"

"I'm good," she replied. "You? How is business going?" It was an awkward question, and Lucy felt herself cringe inside when she asked.

Richard simply nodded, then they fell into another moment of awkward silence before he tipped his head to the side. "I should get these to the counter," he said, pointing behind her.

"Yeah, you should." She side-stepped him so he could roll his cart past her, but he stopped in his tracks.

"For what it's worth, I didn't mean to be a jerk to you. I guess we just don't have the same take on this situation."

Lucy nibbled on her lower lip. An ache spread through her heart at his words, and even though she had concluded earlier in her mind that her relationship with Richard was over, it still didn't make it any easier.

"I know," she answered. "I respect your take… But this is something I must do, regardless of your opinion."

"I believe you will do great, Lucy. You should know that… for what it's worth," he said, repeating the phrase.

"Sure… See you around."

She turned to watch him walk away with his cart and exhaled. That was the most awkward conversation she had ever had, and she was glad it didn't last long.

Lucy hoped they could one day relate with ease again, but right now, she didn't need anyone discouraging her about her choices.

She rounded up her shopping, paid for her items, and headed to the hospital to check on Thelma, as she had promised.

She greeted the doctor who treated Aunt Tricia at the ward's entrance, and another familiar nurse as she passed the nurse's station, drawing closer to Thelma's unit.

Lucy stopped in her tracks when she saw Judy standing by Thelma's bed, knee-deep in the conversation they were having. She wasn't far off from the bed so she could hear Judy clearly when she said. "I did it for you, Thelma. You should know by now that I would let no one walk all over you like that. No one can do that to my precious daughter and get away with it. I told you not to take that deal, but you didn't listen. Now look what it caused."

"It wasn't your choice to make, mom," Thelma countered fiercely, the tone of her voice attracting the attention of a few others around them. "That deal was a once in a lifetime opportunity. I had to take it... you don't know what it's like to be in my shoes, so you don't get to tell me what to do," Thelma argued. "You always ruin everything, just like you did with dad. If you hadn't told him about me, then maybe he'd still be here today."

"Watch it, young lady," Judy countered, forming a fist with her right hand at her side.

Lucy's first instinct as she watched the scene was to continue towards them.

This is probably a family issue, she thought, observing the tense stance Judy assumed when Thelma mentioned her father.

It's best I don't interrupt. She spun around and walked away before either of them noticed her.

22

The next morning, Lucy was still replaying the scene between Thelma and her mother in her head. She was slicing some carrots for the salad she wanted to make, and the kettle on the stove sizzled, reminding her she had put water there to boil.

She turned off the stove, then returned to the table to continue her slicing. Her aunt was still asleep as it was not yet dawn, but Lucy had a lot to prepare. She had moved the basic baking ingredients to her parents' home with Aunt Tricia's help the previous evening, and now all she had to do was bake.

Lucy finished preparing the items for the salad, and she was mixing it all up with cream when Aunt Tricia finally came down the stairs.

"Good morning," Lucy greeted her with a smile as she entered the kitchen. "Did you sleep well?"

"Of course, I did. It's been years since I was last in this house. I've forgotten how cozy it can get, and if not for my alarm, I would have slept the morning away."

Lucy chuckled at that. She offered Aunt Tricia a bowl of salad and set a glass of water in front of her before settling to eat hers. She had whipped up a coffee cake batter first thing when she woke up, and the heady aroma of the ground coffee beans filled the atmosphere.

"Yesterday, I dropped by the hospital to check on Thelma's recovery, and I witnessed something unusual," Lucy began when she finished her salad. "She's better, but I overhead her having an argument with Judy, and there was a lot of tension between them."

"What was it about?" Aunt Tricia asked, wiping her lips with her thumb.

"Something about a deal Judy didn't want Thelma to take, and then Thelma mentioned her father. That got Judy worked up, and defensive. Do you have any idea what happened to Judy's husband?"

Aunt Tricia shook her head. "I think he died of a heart attack. I didn't live in town back then, but I heard from your mother. Judy's just looking out for Thelma. Considering how her acting career has panned out, it's only normal for her mother to be concerned about the kinds of deals she makes with agencies."

"What happened to Thelma's career? Isn't she like really famous or something?" Lucy asked, in the dark to what her aunty was saying.

Aunt Tricia shook her head. "Thelma had bad reviews on her last performance that would have buried any aspiring actor's career, and she found it hard to get another role after that."

"Woah… you're kidding," Lucy exclaimed. Her brows knitted together as she listened to her aunt continue about the movie Thelma failed to act properly, and how horrible her scenes were.

"I thought she was a natural," Lucy said. "I didn't know."

"Guess she didn't take her mother's talent. When I was in college, Judy was famous in town for her acting. She starred in many high school plays and local productions in her time. Everyone naturally expected her daughter to follow suit but turns out Thelma wasn't that gifted."

"So that last role almost ruined her acting career?" Lucy asked.

"I guess she's been auditioning for new roles," Aunt Tricia replied. "I don't think her acting skills compare to her mom's."

She recalled Thelma's argument the previous day. *That deal was a once in a lifetime opportunity… I had to take it.*

"You think maybe Judy didn't want her to take the baker role?" Aunt Tricia asked.

"I don't know."

They both fell silent for a minute, then Aunt Tricia spoke again. "Her first role was in a Pete Jenson production. I remember he used to brag about his latest prodigy in his interviews, but things turned sour when the play started running, and it didn't do well. Pete didn't hesitate to dump her and move on to the next star he could find."

"Seems like Pete was a real jerk when he was alive," Lucy commented.

"He was," Aunt Tricia agreed. "The agency that signed her dropped her after that. I remember running into her at a grocery store once when I came to visit your mother. She wore this black hoodie and shades to make sure no one recognized her, and I just thought that it was so sad."

"I think Thelma aims to improve her acting skill," Lucy said. "She's putting in some effort into her new role by interning at my bakery."

"Is she serious about the internship?"

Lucy exhaled. The answer to her aunt's question was a big no because since Thelma started her internship, which was to last a few weeks, she hadn't been of use to Lucy or Hannah. She only came in once so far, and that day nearly ended in disaster.

"She's not been of any help, though," Lucy stated. "I just want to give her some credit and the benefit of the doubt that she will make something out of the internship."

Lucy rose to her feet to clear out the table and wash the dishes as she spoke. When she finished, she hurried to her bedroom, showered, and dressed for the day before feeding Gigi.

She stood in front of the mirror, brushing her hair, while Gigi feasted on the kibbles in her pan. "Today's going to be a long day, Gigi," Lucy whispered as she tied her hair into a bun on top of her head and brushed away the strands in front to each side of her face.

Aunt Tricia had dressed, and she was ready to join her when she got back downstairs, and they headed out together.

Lucy's first stop was the bakery to check on the progress of the work Keith and his team had already begun.

———

Two days later, Lucy and Hannah were chatting by their stand as the day drew to a close. Lucy adjusted the sleeves of her shirt as Hannah packed the rest of the treats they had left for the day.

Keith came out of the bakery wearing his work overall, and he smiled at Lucy when he got to her small stand near the curb.

"My workers loved the pie you shared," he said.

"Thank you, Keith. I'm glad they enjoyed it," she replied, smiling. "How much more work needs to be done? Can I come in and look?"

"Sure."

Lucy followed him into the bakery, with Hannah behind them. Her jaw dropped in astonishment when she saw the new ceiling boards and the lovely eccentric chandelier light already installed in the middle of the dining area.

They had piled the chairs up in one corner, and the stairs that would lead to the upper level were already in construction.

"This is lovely," Hannah said.

"Yes, it is. Now I can't wait to re-open in this new bakery setting," Lucy agreed.

"It won't be long now," Keith answered. "Let's give it a week or two and we should be finished."

"Alright."

Lucy went on a brief tour around with Hannah and they were discussing the new look when they went outside to join Aunt Tricia.

"Today we had more sales than I had in the entire week. I'm glad things are getting back to normal again," she said.

"Yeah, me too," Hannah said.

They stopped talking when a car pulled to a halt by the curb. Lucy watched and saw Thelma get down. She got to them with quick strides and took the free seat at the table.

"How are you?" Lucy asked. "When were you discharged?"

Thelma beamed at her, and Lucy wondered if Thelma or Judy had seen her at the hospital yesterday before she left.

"I'm alright… thanks for looking out for me, Lucy," Thelma replied. "They discharged me yesterday after all the check-ups."

"Thank goodness, you're alright," Lucy said. She saw Thelma's eyes drift towards Hannah, who had been quiet since Thelma arrived.

"Thanks, Hannah, for going to the hospital with me," Thelma whispered. "If you hadn't been on the scene, then I would have probably been alone the entire time."

Lucy saw Hannah's tentative smile before she replied. "I would have done the same for anyone else," Hannah replied.

For the first time, Hannah didn't frown when Thelma spoke to her, and to Lucy that was a good sign they could one day reconcile their differences.

When Thelma left, Lucy turned to Aunt Tricia and spoke. "I don't think she knows I overheard the argument with her mother yesterday. It's better that way, but something tells me there's more to the argument I witnessed."

"Just be careful, Lucy," Aunt Tricia advised.

"I will. You have nothing to worry about, trust me."

23

On a Sunday morning, Lucy went for a jog to start the day. She stopped after a mile, put her hands on her knees to exhale and relax a bit. The morning breezed wafted through her nose and tickled the skin at the back of her neck. She marveled at it, thankful that spring was drawing ever near.

Her usual route was down Easton Street towards the gas station that led to a bend where she could connect with the high road. When she lived in the apartment above her bakery, she usually jogged in the opposite direction of the route she jogged that morning. That way, she ended her exercise at the end of Easton Street, then walked back to the bakery.

Lucy stretched her legs, straightened her spine and resumed her jog. She made it a few blocks away from her resting point before she saw Tim Humphrey coming out of an adjoining street.

He spotted her too, and paused in his stride, jogging on a spot till she got to him.

"Good morning, Tim," Lucy said. "You jog down this route often?" she asked, wiping her forehead dry as he rotated his arm.

"Yes," he replied. "I live not too far from here, and it is the perfect route for me. What about you? You live around here?"

"On Easton Street, yes," she replied.

"Oh, great."

Lucy looked around them for a second and brought her gaze back to Tim.

"It's a good thing I ran into you. I planned to drop by your bakery to apologize for the last time we saw each other at Judy's shop. I wasn't my best self that day, and I realized I've been grumpy on the two occasions we met. It has nothing to do with my usual personality and everything to do with how life has been for me. It seems being out of work really affects me," Tim said. He shoved his fingers through his dark hair as he spoke, and his eyes landed on Lucy's again. "My apologies, Lucy."

"No problem," she replied, gesticulating with her right hand. "I understand… not being able to work in the theater these past weeks must have been frustrating for you."

"It really is," Tim continued. "I used to enjoy having to handle the preparations for rehearsals or productions, and watching the show was a source of entertainment. I can't do any of that now that the production has been shut down."

"You were a part of the productions?" Lucy asked, not bothering to hide her surprise.

"Yes, yes… I'm not just the janitor," he replied. "Pete and I used to organize rehearsals and produce the plays in town before he had his big break on Broadway. We were a team, and our productions always attracted large audiences. Some of our plays were turned into TV shows and films. But I was never compensated."

"Why is that?"

He shrugged, and his voice dropped a notch as he answered. "Pete never mentioned he had a partner. He's done stuff like that before to a few locals. You help him with something, and he takes all the glory to himself."

Lucy fell silent as she listened to Tim speak. She didn't miss the hint of jealousy in his tone as he continued about how Pete continued using most ideas from their work together to enhance his career, completely forgetting all about Tim and their history together.

"It must hurt for you to watch Pete excel on his own," she sympathized. Putting a hand on her forehead, Lucy stroked her brows and pondered on her next question for a second before asking. "During the open rehearsals Pete organized before he died, did you see Judy's daughter Thelma Cousins there to audition? Do you know if she was at the theater the day Pete died?"

"I'm not sure," he replied, his brows knitting together. "Why do you ask? I'm not shocked though. Pete had a thing for casting many characters in his play. It's one thing we never agreed on… he would cast every Tom, Dick or Sally that popped out of every corner and find a role for them, even when he was certain they had no acting talent."

"Perhaps he just wanted to give them a chance," Lucy suggested.

"Nonsense," Tim cut in, his eyes flaring with anger.

A sudden shiver raced up her spine, and she met his blazing eyes as he added. "He thought he was always right, but he wasn't. Sometimes scenes with a lot of characters are difficult to handle and organize. I tried to tell him this even during these open rehearsals, but he completely shut me up and asked me to do my job, which was being the janitor."

Lucy nodded as she took in the deep frown marring Tim's face and the dissatisfaction that was etched in the lines on his forehead. She licked her dry lips. "Is that why you killed him?" she blurted, unable to stop the question from slipping out of her lips.

"What?" Tim growled.

"Did you kill Pete Jenson?"

He scoffed and took a menacing step towards her. "Watch your back, Lucy," he said in a dangerously low voice. "Don't go around asking stupid questions or digging into matters that don't concern you. It's how you'll get yourself killed."

His threat rang deep in her, and she remained rooted to a spot as he turned away and continued his jog down the road. Lucy blinked, ushering herself back to reality after being stunned at his swift change of character.

She turned to continue into the adjoining street opposite where she stood, still dazed, and the loud blaring honk of a car's horn jarred her out of her thoughts.

Lucy screamed and her hand flew to her chest. She stumbled to the ground by the car that nearly hit her as the door opened and a young man dressed in a prim, black fitted suit stepped out.

"I'm so sorry," he said as he walked over to her and extended his hand. "Are you alright? You seem pretty out of it, and I had to honk that loud to get your attention."

Lucy exhaled. She swallowed, trying to steady her heartbeat by taking slow breaths. The scene reminded her of when a car nearly hit her the previous year.

"I'm alright… I'm fine, I'm not hurt."

"Sorry about this," the man said again. "I'm Joseph Hiller," he added. He reached into his suit pocket; he handed her a card. "I'm going to be the resident producer at the local theater."

"Lucy Hale," she replied. "I own Sweet Delights, a bakery here in Ivy Creek. Nice to meet you."

Joseph Hiller gave her a full smile. He adjusted the lapel of his suit and looked around them. "Care for a ride? I could take you to your destination before continuing to the theater. I don't mind, and it will be a way to apologize for almost knocking you down."

Lucy looked at him, and his smile widened. His green eyes danced as he looked at her.

"Please, don't say no," he said.

Lucy agreed to the offer with a soft nod of her head, and he led her around to the front passenger's seat and held the door open for her to get in before he returned to the driver's seat.

She directed him to take the turn leading into the main street and sat in silence as he drove.

"What production will you be working on?" she asked.

"We hope to bring Pete's production back to life. Because of the ongoing investigation, we'll have to bide our time."

"Sounds like you really believe in Pete's production."

"Pete was like a mentor. He laid the groundwork, and my team and I will finish it in his memory. He was a very talented man, and he deserves to be recognized for his contribution."

Joseph slowed down when they reached the bakery and said, "I'm guessing this is your bakery," he said, pointing at the sign.

"Yes, it is. Thanks for driving me, Mr. Hiller. Really appreciate it."

"It's Joseph and you're welcome. You're one pretty lady, Miss Hale and you should be careful when on the road next time."

Lucy thanked him again and got out of the car. She watched Joseph drive away before she turned and headed for the bakery. It was Sunday, and she was only there because she needed to pick up some baking soda and foil wraps for her round of baking tomorrow morning.

After grabbing the items she needed, Lucy started her walk back to her house. She hummed a popular classical song to herself as she walked, moving her head to the rhythm as she sang. She was enjoying the melody when the blares of oncoming sirens filled the air.

Two cop patrol cars dashed past her, leaving gusts of fumes in their wake.

She stared after the next van that passed, her curiosity spiking when she saw the cops lined up in the open back of the truck.

Something must have happened, she thought. The sirens became distant as they drove farther away from her, leaving Lucy wondering who they were out to arrest.

Have they found who killed Pete Jenson?

24

On Monday morning, Lucy and Aunt Tricia brought out the pastries for sale, arranged them on the display counter by her makeshift stand, and sat under the shade they had created for themselves. She got the first text from Hannah thirty minutes after they settled down to wait for customers for the morning.

> **I won't make it to the bakery today. Something came up at home, and I must take my sister for an appointment. I'll tell you all about it when I get back.**

"Hannah's not coming in today," she said to Aunt Tricia when she raised her head again.

"Is she alright?" Aunt Tricia asked with concern.

"Yes, she's fine… she says something came up with her sister," Lucy replied. She sighed and slipped her phone into the pocket of the apron she wore over her dress. "That leaves us both to handle everything for the day. It's a good thing we have little to do. Keith and his team will be here soon and once they are done for the day, we can close up early and go back home."

Aunt Tricia agreed with her. They spent the next few minutes talking, and Lucy mentioned seeing the cops drive downtown the previous day on her way back from the bakery.

"That was after my run in with the new producer at the theater, Joseph Hiller," she said.

"Do you feel they caught someone? If they did, then news will be all over the local stations already."

"I do," Lucy responded. She rubbed her jaw as she considered any other possibility for the cops to descend on the town in their numbers on a Sunday morning.

Maybe it's an unrelated case?

She was still contemplating the workable options when Aunt Tricia tapped her hand on the table, drawing her attention. "It's Taylor," Aunt Tricia said when Lucy met her gaze.

Lucy looked up to see Taylor approach where they sat with a smile. Lucy rose to her feet to greet him, and he took off the cap on his head.

Taylor ran his fingers through his hair as he spoke. "Hey Lucy, how's it going?"

"Great," she beamed. "How are you, Taylor?"

"Good, good." Taylor greeted Aunt Tricia with a wave of his hand and answered a few questions about his mother before Lucy led him to her stand near the curb.

"I see the workers are making progress," he commented when he stood in front of her and slipped his hands into his back pocket.

Lucy glanced at the bakery's building. "Yes, the workers are yet to get here for the day, but they should be here any minute now."

When she looked back at him again, she noticed he was looking at her. His eyes searched hers for a second before he spoke again. "So, when it's all done, you'll have a bigger dining area, and what else?"

Lucy took time to give him a description of what the bakery would look like on completion.

"That sounds great, Lucy. When it's all done, you should celebrate with a launch party. You deserve it."

"Thanks, Taylor." A thought suddenly flashed across her mind, which she knew Taylor might help with. "I noticed some cops drove down the street yesterday. It looked like they were in a hurry to get somewhere. Did something happen in town?"

"We have a few suspects in Pete's murder case," Taylor replied.

She gasped in surprise.

"It's nothing concrete yet. Yesterday was just a search after getting a warrant."

She was about to ask if the suspect was Tim Humphrey, but he wagged a finger at her. "I can't mention any names, but you have to be careful with whom you are in contact. We've been investigating those who worked at the theater, and the actors who auditioned that day. Some fingerprints besides

Pete's were found on the shirt Pete wore that day, and soon we'll match it with some fingerprints we have on our database."

"Hmmm," she whispered, a shiver racing through her at the thought of the killer possibly being found soon. "I hope it's all wrapped up soon," she continued. "Nearly everyone has been on edge since Pete's death and catching the killer will normalize things."

"You're right," Taylor said.

They both fell silent for a second, and she heard him take in a deep breath before pointing at the cupcakes she had on the counter. "I will have some of that, and three brownies too."

"Sure."

Lucy handed him the paper bag as her phone buzzed in her pocket. "Oh, excuse me."

The text was from Thelma, and she shook her head as she read through it.

> **Hey Lucy, how're things going? I won't be coming in today. I thought I should let you know.**

Lucy typed her reply quickly, tired of allowing Thelma the space to make up excuses and not take her internship seriously. She had given her the weekend off after her accident, and the morning was already far spent before she came up with this excuse.

> **Take all the time you need. You also shouldn't bother resuming tomorrow.**

When she looked up at Taylor again, he was watching her closely.

"That was my intern, Thelma Cousins," she said as she tucked the phone away. "She keeps making excuses not to come to work, and I just can't handle her anymore, so it's best she doesn't work here at all."

Taylor put a hand on her shoulder, surprising her. "Take it easy," he said, his eyes warm on hers. "I should get back home now."

"See you later," she said.

She joined Aunt Tricia again, and minutes later, Keith and his team arrived for the day's work. Lucy and Aunt Tricia attended to the customers that trooped by throughout the day. The day went by without incident and Lucy was glad when she noticed it was almost time to close for the day.

Lucy had taken in her stand and was closing the windows when she saw Judy approach the bakery. Judy walked with quick strides, glancing over her shoulder briefly.

"Good evening, Judy," Lucy greeted as she stepped out to greet Judy at the entrance.

"Lucy," she said in an icy tone as she adjusted the shoulder bag hanging loosely on her left hand. "Were you locking up?'

"Ah, yes… I was just leaving for the day," Lucy replied. "Do you want to buy some treats? I still have some left."

Judy shook her head. "No, no, I'm not here for some treats, Lucy. I'm here to see you, and it's quite urgent, so may I come in?"

Judy pushed past her and entered the bakery as she asked, and Lucy followed.

She wondered what Judy's visit was for as she closed the door behind her and walked past Judy to where her previous display counter stood. "What did you need?" Lucy asked, crossing her hands over her chest as she met Judy's gaze.

The corner of Judy's lips lifted into a crooked smirk as she answered, "I saw you at the hospital that day… I know you were there."

25

Lucy froze where she stood as Judy continued. "I saw you right before you turned and hurried out."

"I..." Lucy's words died in her throat when Aunt Tricia appeared on the stairway, beaming as usual.

"Judy," Aunt Tricia called in a singing voice, her eyes opened wide as she descended the stairs and hugged Judy. "It's been ages since I last saw you. Oh, my goodness," she exclaimed, laughing as Judy hugged her back. "How have you been? Look at you, you're... Different."

"I'm alright, Tricia," Judy responded, giggling as she hugged Aunt Tricia again.

Lucy swallowed. The ice she had heard in Judy's tone a moment earlier had completely disappeared, and she wondered if she had imagined it. Her palms had turned sweaty, and she closed her eyes, told herself Judy wasn't here to attack her before opening them again.

"I was telling Lucy the other day about how you used to be Meryl Streep back in school. You would have made a fantastic actress. How come you never pursued that?" Aunt Tricia asked. She still held Judy's hand in hers as she talked, and Lucy backed away from them into the kitchen to make sure the back doors were locked.

"Life happened," Judy replied as Lucy walked away. "I met my husband, got married, had Thelma and the rest, as they say, is history. I have no regrets, though. I have a wonderful flower shop that serves Ivy Creek and beyond. My daughter's doing well with her acting career. I get to help our town as a member of the town council. I love my life."

"Amazing… Lucy gave me a bouquet she bought from your store, and they were really therapeutic. I loved them so much."

"I'm glad you did, Tricia," Judy replied.

Inside the kitchen, Lucy switched off the lights after admiring the progress of the work for a while. When she got back to the dining area, Aunt Tricia and Judy were still catching up, and she waited, her hands behind her back.

"It was nice seeing you again after all these years," Judy said as Aunt Tricia pulled away from her.

"Same here, Judy… I need to run along now. I have an appointment. See you around soon."

Lucy caught Aunt Tricia's gaze as she backed away, and Judy faced her again.

Aunt Tricia walked out of the bakery, and Lucy sucked in a deep breath as she looked at Judy.

"Your aunt was a good friend of mine when we were in college. I haven't seen her in years and it feels good to reunite with an old friend."

Judy's tone held a wistfulness that was charming, but she was more concerned with the reason for Judy's visit.

"I saw you at the hospital with Thelma, and I didn't want to interfere, so I left," she said, causing Judy to arch a brow as she looked at her.

"Fine, but that's not why I'm here, Lucy."

"Then why?"

Judy took off her bag and set it on the ground gently. "I've had a very busy day, but I had to stop what I was doing when Thelma called and mentioned you fired her."

Lucy blinked. "I can't have Thelma working here," she replied after a moment. "She's not dedicated to learning, and honestly, she's just not cut out for this kind of work. It's best she tries to do something else she will be good at."

Judy put her hands together in front of her. She then massaged her temples and looked at Lucy again. "I beg you, Lucy," she said, coming closer. Her blue eyes searched Lucy's desperately, and she lurched forward to grab Lucy's hands. "She needs this… I need this. The role Thelma got is a once in a lifetime opportunity and I did a lot to get her that spot in the production. It'll be a stepping stone to bigger and better things," she said. "She needs to do this," she added in a hoarse voice, spacing her words to sound convincing. "Please…"

Lucy dragged her hands from Judy's. "I can't do that, Judy," she said. "Thelma's clumsy… the incident with Stephanie affected sales and damaged my reputation. I'm yet to recover from that and I can't afford a worker who isn't of help."

"Thelma can be of help," she rushed to add.

"But she's not. She's not helping, and she's certainly not learning. I thought I could put up with her attitude, but I really can't, and I don't want any trouble, Judy. It's best she finds someplace else to intern."

Lucy turned away from Judy but stopped when Judy clamped a hand on her arm and spun her back around.

Judy's lower lip quivered as she stared at Lucy. Her eyes turned watery, and for a second Lucy thought she was about to cry.

"I gave so much to get her to where she is, but she's never able to keep up. I've spent so much on acting classes, dance glasses… I even hired a teacher to teach her Spanish in case a role came up in the Spanish-speaking world. Everyone remembers her as the kid in the toothpaste commercial, but she has so much more to offer. This role she's got is her ticket out of this town. I know Thelma can be a spoiled brat, but I know if she applies herself, she can be good… maybe great. I suggested she come and intern with you as nothing beats living and breathing a role."

Lucy rubbed the back of her neck and sighed. "I can't do what you want, Judy. I'm so sorry, but this is my business on the line, too. Thelma almost ruined it, and I can't give her another chance."

Judy sneered. She turned away from Lucy and began pacing, one hand on her hip and the other on her forehead. "This is all his fault and now, even after his death, we still can't recover from the havoc he caused."

"Judy..." Lucy began.

Judy's head snapped up, and she took menacing steps towards Lucy, who staggered backwards and collided with a table behind her.

"I begged Pete to give her a chance, just like I'm begging you, Lucy. He was just too stuck up to see that she's talented… just like you."

"Judy…" Lucy began. Her eyes widened as Judy stopped in front of her.

"You, Lucy of all people, should know that everyone needs a second chance. Look at how much progress you've made with your business. I'm sure you came this far because you had support from others and all I'm asking is that you give Thelma that same support. She really needs to excel in this role. It's her dream."

Judy's tone had regained the same chill it had earlier when she entered. Her face had paled and now she was giving Lucy a crazed look that made Lucy's mouth dry up. Her chest rose and fell with the force of her breathing as she asked. "Thelma's dreams? Or yours?"

The question made Judy back away from Lucy for a while, and suddenly she burst into a full cackle that filled the room.

Lucy saw sweat beads on Judy's forehead. Her eyes were red as she sneered at Lucy.

"She's my daughter," she started through gritted teeth. "Her dreams are mine… and… My dreams are hers. I would do anything to see her shine like she's supposed to." Judy scratched her forehead and added. "Even if it means getting stumbling blocks like yourself out of the way."

The threatening words set alarm bells in Lucy's head off. She dashed for the door, intending to breeze past Judy's side and get to it, but Judy was faster. Judy's firm hands grabbed Lucy's ponytail, and she yanked hard, dragging Lucy back to her.

"It took little to end Pete, and I'd do it all over again if I got the chance," Judy was saying as she tightened her grip. "And it won't take much to end you, too."

Judy's hands came around Lucy's neck, squeezing until Lucy felt like she was going to pass out.

Her skin flushed, her chest deflated, and she struggled, holding onto the last chunk of air she had inside her. Lucy held on to Judy's crazed gaze as she fought to hold on to her consciousness. An eerie feeling of déjà vu crept over her as, once again, she was in a battle to stay alive.

26

The blares of sirens filled the air as Lucy fought to free herself from Judy's firm grasp.

Her eyelids fluttered closed as she looked at Judy one last time. Lucy's hands clamped over Judy's wrists, and she tried to break free again at the same time Judy let go of her and rushed for the door.

Lucy scrambled away from Judy. Her hands moved to her neck, and she swallowed against the burning sensation rising in her chest. The door swung open just as Judy was about to run out, and cops came barging into the bakery. Lucy saw her stagger backwards and make a run for the kitchen, but she was too late.

The cops surrounded Judy. One of them grabbed her hands and cuffed her wrists behind her before she could run. Aunt Tricia entered the bakery and ran towards Lucy to hold her.

"Are you alright, honey?" Aunt Tricia asked. "Did she hurt you badly?"

Lucy managed a nod. She didn't think the lump in her throat would let her speak, and frankly, her dazed brain couldn't form any words.

Grateful for support when Aunt Tricia put a hand around her waist, Lucy leaned into her body; her breaths kept coming out in strained puffs as she watched them drag Judy away.

"I'll make you pay for this, Lucy. I swear I'll make you pay," Judy cursed, and tried to free herself from the cop's grip. "I will make sure you pay… I'll kill you, Lucy, just like I killed Pete," she continued, laughing hysterically.

"She's completely unhinged," Aunt Tricia murmured at Lucy's side, shaking her head.

"She's crazy," Lucy murmured as she slumped to the ground. Her backside contacted the floor with a loud thud, and her shoulders slumped as she exhaled. Taylor appeared at the doorway, and she met his gaze as he hurried towards her.

"Are you alright?" He asked, his hands coming around her. He pulled her in, one hand patting her hair and the other rubbing her back. "You're safe now. I'm here and you're safe," he said.

Lucy shuddered and allowed herself the liberty to enjoy the warmth of his comfort. She closed her eyes as he brushed tendrils of hair away from the side of her head and helped her to her feet.

"Oh, Lucy," Aunt Tricia called as she returned to the bakery. "I just gave my statement to the cops," she said, coming closer to take Lucy out of Taylor's embrace. "It's a good thing I hung around and called the cops immediately."

"Yes," Taylor replied. "Judy did not know you were still around. That's how Lucy got lucky."

Taylor looked at her as he spoke. He rubbed his chin for a second before adding. "Once the paramedics get here, they'll assess you and determine if you need to go to the hospital."

"That'll be unnecessary," Lucy said, finally finding her voice again. Her throat still hurt, the skin there burned, and she had to keep her hands against the section that hurt. "I'm fine. I don't need to go to the hospital."

"You're not fine," Taylor and Aunt Tricia chorused.

"Your neck and cheeks are all blotched, and you need to get checked," Taylor said.

His hands were on his waist as he spoke, and he looked around the bakery. The door opened and two paramedics entered. Aunt Tricia brought Lucy a chair to sit on and Lucy snuggled into the blanket the paramedics wrapped around her shoulders before a cop came to question her.

She told him everything that had happened. Judy's consistent begging to give Thelma her job back and the dramatic change in her behavior when Lucy had refused. By the time she finished, and the cops excused themselves, Lucy turned to see Taylor standing near the entrance to the bakery. He stood with his back to her, his attention completely engrossed in the conversation he was having with the cop next to him.

With a sigh, she tried to get on her feet, but gasped when she swooned and nearly fell to the ground. Taylor hurried to her side and steadied her with both hands.

"You should come with me to the hospital," he said, this time hooking her arm in his and turning her towards the door.

"I'm fine," Lucy insisted. "I have Aunt Tricia here, and she will be with me at the house tonight, Taylor."

"It's not enough," he argued just as Aunt Tricia entered the bakery again.

"The paramedics are waiting," Aunt Tricia said, letting them through the door. Lucy didn't put up any more fight as Taylor helped her into the van with her aunt's help. She lay on the stretcher there, sighing as her body relaxed against it.

Her head still spun from what just happened, and even though she wasn't physically hurt, Lucy knew she needed time to wrap her mind around her near death experience. Taylor had saved her again, and she was thankful for that.

Lucy's eyes closed as the ambulance door closed. Her aunt sat by her side, so she could relax. The next time she opened her eyes, her heart was trembling inside her chest. She sat up with the rush of adrenaline that filled her. Her eyes took in her surroundings, and the surge subsided when she remembered she was at the hospital.

Hannah came into the room then, a soft smile on her face as she opened the door.

"Hey," she whispered, coming close to Lucy's bed to hug her. "Aunt Tricia already filled me in... Who would have suspected that Judy was one crazy lady?"

"I can't still believe it myself," Lucy replied, allowing herself to get squashed into Hannah's tight embrace. "Turns out she's controlling and manipulative."

"Taylor was here earlier, and he told me everything," Aunt Tricia said. "Judy became hysterical once they got to the station. She confessed to killing Pete because he refused to give Thelma a lead role in his new play. She hadn't meant to kill him when she disguised as one of the actors in the stampede scene, but she considered it sweet revenge when she found out he had died."

"The news already has reports on this, and Judy's picture is pasted across every media outlet. There's no way she'll get out of this without a maximum sentence," Hannah added. "The police matched a stain of Pete's blood to a hoodie found in the basement of Judy's house after a thorough search."

Lucy and Hannah continued talking about Judy for a few more minutes till Aunt Tricia came into the room with Taylor right beside her.

"Ah, you're awake," she exclaimed, beaming as she walked over to Lucy and enveloped her in a hug.

Taylor grinned as he stood at the door with his arms crossed over his chest. "The doctors confirmed that you're fine, but we insisted you stay the night on bed rest. It was unanimous," she said, pointing at Taylor and Hannah. "So, you're not getting out of it."

"Okay," Lucy replied, grinning. She was thankful for life and didn't want to argue with anyone for now. She had people to support her, so she was fine.

Hannah and Aunt Tricia left her in the room with Taylor, and he crossed over to the bed and sat on its side. "It's all over now. Judy will get the justice she deserves, and now you can go back to business and baking," he said, his eyes not leaving hers.

"It's finally over," she repeated, her words ending on a sigh.

A minute of silence passed between them, and Taylor rose to his feet, patted her hair away from her face tenderly, and turned to walk away.

"Thank you," Lucy said.

He stopped and faced her again, his lips curving into a smile that reached his eyes. "For saving my life every time," she said, her voice rich with emotion.

"You're welcome," he replied. "Stay safe, Lucy."

Lucy watched him walk away, and her heart filled with a slow flutter as the image of his smile registered in her head. When she angled her head to one side, she saw Aunt Tricia and Hannah standing by the room's shutter windows, giggling as they watched her.

27

THREE WEEKS LATER

*L*ucy clinked her glass with Hannah's, and then Aunt Tricia's, before sipping her sparkling grape juice.

"Cheers," the three women chorused and drank again, then Lucy turned on the music playing on the speaker, flung her head back and danced to the rhythm of the song playing.

"Tell us, how did it go with the health inspector?" Aunt Tricia asked when they sat down after the first song had ended.

Lucy picked up her fork to cut into her steak, and Hannah filled her plate with some mushroom sauce.

She had prepared that Sunday lunch to celebrate their new success. The renovations were complete, and the overall look was brilliant. Lucy especially loved the patterned floorboards compared to the regular brown ones her parents had installed when they first bought the building.

The walls were now a blend of pastel colors; there was a spacious aisle between every table set-up to avoid congestion, and her kitchen felt wider because it had more space considering they had removed the wooden walls demarcating it from the dining area and expanded it.

"I passed the check and I'm looking forward to a more fruitful spring," she replied, beaming at her aunt as she took the first bite of her steak.

Their discussion continued over lunch. Lucy had given Hannah the weekend off after they had arranged the bakery, and tomorrow was the start of a new business era for her. She was yet to take pictures of the overall outlook, but that was something she could do sometime later.

Aunt Tricia and Hannah were going over the new flower vase on the front porch when the bell rang and Thelma entered the bakery. Everyone around the table fell silent as she approached, and Lucy stood up first to greet her.

"Hi, Lucy," Thelma said in a shaky voice. Her eyes were wide, and beneath them, Lucy noticed large dark circles. "You look good."

Lucy offered her a seat, noticing how she clung to the shoulder bag she carried. Thelma twisted the hem of the blazer she wore as she looked around the bakery. Hannah cleared her throat and lifted her glass to her lips. Lucy met Hannah's questioning gaze before she turned her attention to Thelma again.

"I thought I should drop by to congratulate you," Thelma began, nibbling on her lower lip when Lucy didn't break eye contact. "I heard about the renovation… everyone in town is wondering what the new look is like, and I think it's lovely."

"Thank you, Thelma. How have you been?"

Thelma lifted a shoulder in a shrug. "I've been holding up, trying to keep my head up amidst everything else."

She didn't need to get into explicit details for Lucy to know what she was referring to. Judy's court hearing ended in a week because all evidence had pointed to her. Coupled with her threatening Lucy's life, and her confession as the cops dragged her away, it was already over before it began.

Seeing Thelma now made Lucy feel sorry for her. It must have been hard trying to live with a mother like Judy who controlled everything about her life, she thought.

"I'm really sorry, Lucy. For what my mother did, and for…" Thelma's voice trailed off before she finished the sentence, and a heavy log of pity for her formed in Lucy's chest.

"You shouldn't apologize," she spoke and reached out a hand to take Thelma's. "I know you're sorry, and it's all over now. Everyone's moving on, and you should do so, too."

"I'm trying to," Thelma said, releasing an unexpected laugh. "But it's hard to do that when everyone in town keeps murmuring whenever I pass. I'm leaving for a while. There's a photography internship in Denver I got into, and I plan to be serious with this one."

"Is photography what you want? Is it your dream?"

"Yes, it always has been. When I mentioned to my mother that I took the internship, she didn't want me to go. I told her it was a once in a lifetime opportunity, but she thought it was mediocre and nothing compared to what I could be if I was an actress. There's nothing stopping me from taking that path now."

"There isn't," Lucy agreed, smiling at her. "I want you to do what your heart wants because that's the only way you will be happy."

Thelma nodded. She spoke to Hannah and Aunt Tricia for a while and by the time Lucy walked her to the door; they hugged goodbye before she walked away. Lucy didn't re-enter the bakery immediately because she spotted Taylor's car parked across the street from her building.

He got out, crossed the road, and walked to her, holding a bouquet of daisies in one hand.

"You look amazing," he said when he got to where Lucy stood and handed her the flowers. "I also remembered how much you love daisies."

"Thank you," she replied, grinning at him.

She had invited him for the celebratory lunch, and although he was a bit late, she was still glad he made it, anyway.

"Thanks for coming," she said, stepping aside to let him into the bakery.

"I wouldn't miss celebrating with you for anything in the world."

He entered the bakery and moved to Aunt Tricia, hugging her lightly before greeting Hannah and taking a free seat at the table.

Lucy took the flowers into her office, set them in a vase, then joined them at the dining area again to make another toast. The afternoon spanned into an evening full of laughter and joy after their lunch, and Lucy stole glances at Taylor as he conversed with Hannah and her aunt.

When the year started, she had been so full of hope, and she felt a renewed surge of that energy fill her again as the peaceful sounds of their laughter tickled her ears. Lucy was looking forward to what Ivy Creek's spring offered.

The End

AFTERWORD

Thank you for reading Waffles and Scuffles. I really hope you enjoyed reading it as much as I had writing it!

If you have a minute, please consider leaving a review on Amazon or the retailer where you got it.

Many thanks in advance for your support!

WHICH PIE GOES WITH MURDER?

CHAPTER 1 SNEAK PEEK

CHAPTER 1 SNEAK PEEK

The town hadn't changed much since Lucy's last visit. She noticed this when she arrived at the cemetery earlier that day for her parent's funeral. It was a short ceremony, and she had made most of the plans together with her aunt while she was in Ivy Creek. When she arrived earlier that morning, she had gone straight to the cemetery.

Her aunt drove back to her house in the neighboring town as soon as the ceremony was over, and Lucy headed back home. The first thing Lucy noticed as she arrived at her parent's house was that the front lawn was still as beautifully kept as ever. Her mother had always paid special attention to it. She had loved the beautiful burst of flowers that bloomed, especially in the summer, and Lucy had grown to love that effect too.

She got out of her car and looked around the yard, unable to wrap her mind around the death of her parents. It was sudden, painful, and destabilizing. It'd been a few days, but she already missed them.

This town, Ivy Creek, was not a place for her, and she hoped she wouldn't have to stay in town for a day longer than necessary. She had moved to the city years ago, where she had carved out a life for herself, and she was thriving there. This tragedy was the only thing bringing her back to town.

As she walked towards the front door of the house, she turned around when she heard a dog bark. She saw the next-door neighbor, Maureen Jones, a woman Lucy remembered from when she was little, walk past holding her dog on a leash.

"Lucy, dear," the woman's edgy voice boomed, the corners of her lips lifted in a smile.

Lucy forced a smile onto her face and turned around to greet Maureen.

"It's a surprise to see you in town, and a tragedy what happened to your parents. They were such a lovely couple."

Lucy greeted her with a peck on both cheeks and stepped back.

"I hope you are handling everything fine?"

"Yes, I am," she replied with another smile. "Thank you, Mrs. Jones."

The woman nodded and pulled on the leash of her dog as she walked away. Lucy turned around and walked to the house. She went right to the flower pot at the corner of the front porch, took the keys from under it, and slipped it into the keyhole to open the door.

Once inside, she looked around, and a wave of nostalgia hit her. Tears instantly filled her eyes. The last time she was here, it was Christmas, three years ago. She had made it just in time for the traditional family dinner after her mother had nagged her about it for weeks.

She felt an instant wave of guilt overwhelm her for caring less about her parents these past years. *This is my home. I grew up here, but now it feels different... empty.*

I should have visited more often.

She sucked in a deep breath, headed for the stairs in the corner. Upstairs, Lucy looked around, taking in the perfect arrangements of the smaller living room. The pictures of her when she was younger hanging on the walls, and more of her dad holding her when she had won her first award in high school on the girl's sprinting team.

Lucy wiped at her eyes gently, then took a short tour around the rest of the house. Her old bedroom was still the same, her pictures hung on the wall, and her closet remained untouched. The wallpapers she had loved so much still hung on the walls.

She dropped on the bed, and gently stroked the sheets with her hands, then sniffed. "I'm so sorry mom, and dad. I should have been here more often," she muttered to herself.

In a few hours, she would be hosting guests in the bakery, and she didn't feel like she was up to it, but she dragged herself off the bed. She spent time staring at her reflection in the full-length mirror by the corner of her bed, then went into her closet to find a pair of jeans and a T-shirt that still fit. She grabbed the keys to the bakery from her parent's room and headed out.

The drive to the bakery on one of Ivy Creek's high streets was short. The outside remained the same, with its Norman Rockwell like painting. The inside was arranged in a pattern that drew the customers to the right side where the display glasses were, and a huge menu hung on the wall, listing everything they made. Minutes later, she was inside, cleaning up and gathering baking supplies from the shelves she could use to prepare snacks for her guests. She went into the storage room and came back with everything she needed in a large bowl, then went ahead to prepare a mixture for blueberry streusel muffins and cookies.

Lucy used her mother's recipes she had learned when she was younger. She used to enjoy helping her out in the bakery a lot back then, and watching her parents work together had been fun. It was why she had successfully carved out a career in food blogging for herself and trying out new recipes was a favorite for her.

Lucy sat in the kitchen and waited after putting her dough into the oven. The bakery was still intact, and for a moment, she wondered what would happen now that they were gone. They had put so much effort and dedication into running the bakery for years, and Sweet Delights had thrived because of that.

The creamy and comforting scent of vanilla she had used in her dough filled the atmosphere, alerting her that her muffins were baked into a perfectly brown color, and as she took them out, and put in the next set, a soft knock on the front door told her the first guest had arrived.

IN ABOUT AN HOUR, the bakery was filled with citizens of Ivy Creek, some of whom Lucy recognized. They were all pleasant, chatting lightly amongst themselves as they enjoyed the confectionaries she had baked. She was proud she was able to pull it off in a few hours. Cleaning the bakery hadn't been hard at all as it was hardly ever dirty, and the majority of the work had been baking the pastries.

Lucy greeted an old friend of her father's briefly with a handshake, engaged in a light conversation with him for a few minutes before moving on to anyone else she recognized. Half an hour into the meeting, the door to the bakery opened again, and Lucy's heart did a slow dive in her chest as she noticed the man who walked in through the door. He was dressed in a black shirt tucked into navy blue jeans, and she didn't miss the gun belt on his waist. Lucy knew he had always wanted to go into law enforcement and could see he did it.

She swallowed as his eyes scanned the room, then settled on her. They stared at each other for a brief moment, and the only thing Lucy could think of at that moment was that in the five years since she last saw him, he hadn't changed one bit.

Of course, he had aged a little. His once boyish looks were gone and had been replaced with stubble that covered his face. Their gaze locked for a moment before he walked towards her. Lucy sipped from the glass she held and cleared her throat when he arrived and stood in front of her, slipping his hands into his pocket.

"Lucy Hale," he said in a low voice, his pale blue eyes not leaving hers. "It took a tragedy to bring you back home."

His statement was flat, with an underlying meaning they both understood, and Lucy plastered a smile on her face and extended a hand to him. He hesitated at first, but then slowly accepted the gesture.

"Taylor Baker—it's a pleasant surprise to have you here," she replied, and he cocked a brow. His gaze roamed her face again, and Lucy knew from the look in his eyes that he had not forgotten their history.

Taylor released her hand and slipped his back into his pocket. "Mr. and Mrs. Hale were friends of my parents too, and they are here, so it's only right that I pay my respects."

Lucy nodded, and just then Taylor's mother found them and greeted Lucy with a big hug. "Hello, Mrs. Baker."

"We are so sorry for your loss, dear," Taylor's mother whispered to her and took both her hands in hers. "It's a tragedy what happened to Morris and Kareen. They were such lovely people, the accident was a true loss for every one of us."

"Thank you," Lucy replied gently with a smile again, and Taylor whispered something to his mother before she walked away.

"So, you running again as soon as this is over?" he asked casually. "We both know Ivy Creek does not suit your exquisite needs," he added.

Her mind prepared a snappy reply to his question, but she suppressed it and nodded instead.

She didn't have the strength to get into an argument with Taylor, not at a gathering hosted in honor of her parents. All she wanted was for the night to be over, so she could slip into her bed and sleep for a long time. She was exhausted, partly because she had to stand here and accept condolences from almost everyone in town.

The gathering was her aunt's idea, and she wasn't even here to attend it because she had to get back to her daughter, who just had a baby back home.

"I don't think I'll stay," Lucy replied with a small smile, ignoring the contempt she saw in his eyes.

"I didn't think you would."

Three years ago, the Christmas she had visited, she ran into Taylor at the grocery store, and his attitude had been the same. Even though she had tried to apologize to him then, too. Lucy knew she didn't need to apologize every time they ran into each other. They had shared history, and she had chosen to move on for the sake of her career. If he couldn't forgive her for that, then there was little she could do about it.

"Thanks for paying your respects, Taylor. I appreciate it. I have to go now… to talk to other guests," she said, emptying the contents of her glass as she walked away from him, aware that his gaze was pinned on her the entire time.

She stole glances at him as he moved to join his parents in the corner of the bakery. She saw him join their conversation, and as he picked up one muffin and took a bite, she waited to see the reaction on his face.

He had enjoyed her baking once, when they were together, and he complimented it far too many times. She couldn't tell if he still thought it was good enough, and before she could look away, his gaze found hers across the room again, and lingered. He looked away first, and Lucy turned and focused on the conversation with her guests.

By the end of the gathering, Lucy cleaned up the place alone and finished late. She didn't want to go back to the main house tonight. The place held a lot of memories of her happy life there and it was painful to stay there alone.

She remembered there was a small apartment above the bakery, and as she closed the doors to the main entrance and locked the back exit, she hoped it would come in handy for her for the night. Lucy went up the stairs and flipped the light switch on, and the first thing she saw was her mother's cat, Gigi, huddled in a corner.

She bent over and touched its head as it came towards her. She let her gaze travel around the small living space, and she smiled. "This is better than I remember, and it'll be perfect."

She went in to check the bedrooms; there were two of them. It was more than enough for the night, or as long as she wished to stay. She made a trip downstairs to grab her luggage in her car, parked in the backyard. After closing her doors, she retired back to the living room upstairs to comfort herself with a cup of chamomile tea, hoping it would ease the stress of what had been quite an eventful day.

Seeing the number of locals who turned up in honor of her parents surprised her, and Taylor's presence too had shocked her, but his usual cold attitude hadn't. He was never going to forgive her. She had come to terms with that, and she could handle it.

As Lucy fell asleep, she hoped that time would heal the heaviness in her heart from her loss. When she opened her eyes the next morning, it was to the sound of something clattering downstairs. Lucy jumped out of her bed, and her heartbeat skyrocketed, leaving her with a rush of adrenaline that produced a tight knot in the pit of her stomach.

Who was out there?

WHICH PIE GOES WITH MURDER?

AN IVY CREEK COZY MYSTERY

RUTH BAKER

ALSO BY RUTH BAKER

The Ivy Creek Cozy Mystery Series

Which Pie Goes with Murder? (Book 1)

Twinkle, Twinkle, Deadly Sprinkles (Book 2)

Waffles and Scuffles (Book 3)

Silent Night, Unholy Bites (Book 4)

Waffles and Scuffles (Book 5)

NEWSLETTER SIGNUP

Want **FREE** COPIES OF FUTURE **CLEANTALES** BOOKS, FIRST NOTIFICATION OF NEW RELEASES, CONTESTS AND GIVEAWAYS?

GO TO THE LINK BELOW TO SIGN UP TO THE NEWSLETTER!

https://cleantales.com/newsletter/